Bob Moats

I0567283

Wiseguy
Murders

Copyright © 2014 by Bob Moats.

Rev. 0324141105

1

Wiseguy Murders

For information and address:
Magic 1 Productions
P.O. Box 524, Fraser MI 48026-0524
Website: http://murdernovels.com
Cover by Bob Moats

Bob Moats

Other Jim Richards series books by Bob Moats

For a preview or to purchase a book, go to
http://murdernovels.com

What a few people are saying about Murder Novels by Bob Moats

Mr. Moats, I just got your novel "Classmate Murders" and have to let you know, I read it in one evening. That is the first book I have ever done that with. That was the most enjoyable book I have ever read. I just started reading e-books, and reading again, after getting my wife a Kindle. This book was my 12th, and the best. I just got Las Vegas Showgirls to (read) tomorrow evening. I look forward to reading many of your books in this series. I have been searching for an author and books that were fun, entertaining reads. Your books are just the ticket.

Regards, A new fan, Bill from South Carolina

****

Another very nice comment submitted through my website from Micki P.:

"I recently was given a kindle for my 60th birthday. The first book I downloaded was the Classmate Murders and have now read every one of the them. Today I started on the Fatal Rejection series. Thank you for the wonderful ride with Jim and Penny and all the rest of the troop. I have laughed and giggled thru the stories, my poor family gave me the strangest looks! Now I really want a little Yorkie!! Fatal Rejection so far is another great read! I will be looking out for more of Jim Richards and since you are my #1 Author, anything of yours I can find."

Extra special thanks to:

Special thanks to Val Brooks who edited this book and for her great suggestions.

Thanks to the beta readers Cindy Gross Valstad, Susan Houghton and Al Norris.

Thank you to all the people who purchased this book. I hope you enjoy it as much as I enjoyed writing it for my faithful readers.

The Jim Richards Family of Readers is listed in the back of the book.

Wiseguy Murders by Bob Moats

Chapter 1

Buck and Mac were making another trip around the perimeter of the newly renovated two-story motel, now a shelter for the homeless along with survivors of domestic and sexual violence. Buck's guards were patrolling the grounds due to the occasional fights and minor violence that occurred by the disadvantaged homeless persons who felt others were against them. Most of these people came from the streets or out of the flood tunnels from below the city of Las Vegas and the huge motel converted to a shelter was now a place to get away from the harshness of living in hostile areas. But they still weren't trusting of others and guarded their meager belongings carefully.

When the shelter first opened, it was decided that Buck would have his security guards stationed around the building to help prevent any outbreaks of violence that may occur. The motel was set-up for the safety of the people who lived there, but a lot of the people weren't happy about having to share a room with others.

Reverend Harold Renford was the coordinator of the shelter and since he had many years of experience dealing with the homeless, he knew it was not going to be a totally friendly place. Those persons who were survivors of domestic and sexual violence were separated from the living quarters of the homeless. The DV shelter was administered by a local organization that provided help and shelter to abused spouses and children. They were short of rooms to house all the needy people in their own shelters, so our shelter was offered as an extra place to house the overflow.

Penny and I would visit frequently to see how things were going, since we had spent a good amount of our own money to buy the motel and renovate it. Harold was wealthy and he had been rescued by Trapper, Deacon and me from the clutches of people wanting to steal his money and valuable land property. After we solved the Santa murder case, I convinced Harold to invest in the motel. He was more than happy to help with his generous funding. He also lived on the premises, which helped to maintain his presence with the people. Many knew him from the old church he had before he sold the property to developers who wanted to build more casinos and hotels for the people who didn't have to worry about where their next meal was coming from.

Wiseguy Murders

The big community room in the shelter was converted into a makeshift church for Harold's Sunday worship, and used as a cafeteria to feed the vast number of people who took refuge there. A kitchen was built in the back of the room and served hot meals three times a day. Harold and I had talked to a number of community agencies and wealthy financiers about donating money, food and other necessities to help make the stay at the shelter as pleasant as possible. There were also on-site counselors and job placement personnel to get many of the people back on their feet and out of the shelter into better lives.

Lacey's husband, Mac, was running the security portion of my investigating firm now that Buck was a licensed investigator, and busy with his own cases. I suggested to Mac to get a number of the homeless men involved in a patrol of the property to help keep the peace. That would give them a sense of pride in helping with the daily operations of the shelter and earn a small wage to help them out.

The newest member of my little family, Fred Jarvis, was a big help around the place. Fred had been a homeless person himself, before I helped get him out of the tunnels. He became a valuable part of my firm. He also knew a number of the homeless, many who looked up to him since he made it out of the tunnels—he gave them hope. Fred still had his work to do in our own building—cleaning, lawn care and guarding the building at night—but he would go over to the shelter to help when he could. We got him a car, so he had more freedom to move around.

Buck had time to kill this particular day, so he joined Mac in making the rounds to check on the guards. In one section of the building, they came to a half-opened door to one of the rooms. Mac decided to check and see if everything was all right. He pulled his huge flashlight and shined it into the room, since there were no lights on.

"Hello? Everything all right in there?" Mac called into the room. He glanced at a plaque on the front of the door which had the names written of the people who shared the room. At present, there were only two persons assigned to this room. Buck came up behind Mac and yelled in also. There was no reply. Mac went further into the room and reached to the wall switch, turning the room light on. The overhead light brightened up the room, now painted in bright colors to hopefully cheer up the residents.

There was no one in the room. Mac approached the half-opened bathroom door, and pushed the door open wider. He paused, looked back to Buck and said, "I think we need the police." He moved back so Buck could look in. Buck saw the man hanging by the neck with a rope tied to the shower rod.

~~*~~

Wiseguy Murders

I was visiting Penny at her studio while she was interviewing a famous movie starlet, Lorna Jackson, about a film she had just wrapped up in Vegas. I didn't go to the studio very often, but today I had nothing better to do and I wanted to visit with my wife for once at her place of work. She always came by my office to bug me before having me take her out to get lunch.

Gordy, Penny's producer, came up behind me and I jumped when I saw him. "Sorry, I've learned to move very quietly around the studio while we tape the show," he said with a smile. "What brings you here today? No crimes, I hope." Gordy reached out to ruffle Willy's head as I held the tiny dog.

"No, just slumming. I thought I'd come in to watch Penny do her stuff," I replied.

"Besides looking at Lorna Jackson?"

"Well, she is a big star and not hard on the eyes," I said with a grin.

"Our ratings go up when she's on the show."

"How are the ratings doing? I know the survival of her show is in the ratings."

"Penny's safe, her ratings put her in the top ten of daytime programming. It will take a lot to bump her off," Gordy replied with his chest out. He was proud to have been with Penny from the start, moving with her from the little local cable show back in Michigan. He fought to get her back into a network spot after she quit the first show when she was upset by the way things were handled by management regarding her guests being killed.

"I hope she hangs in there. A happy Penny is a happy Penny," I said with a laugh.

The show ended and the audience was moving out of the studio. Gordy excused himself and went off to do his job. I slowly went back to Penny's dressing room and in to see the flurry of people getting her make-up off and dressed for the day. She saw me in the mirror and waved as I sat and placed Willy next to me. He yipped once seeing her. All the girls in the room laughed at his attempt to call to her.

As I sat, my cell phone buzzed. I debated whether to answer, but I did since the caller ID said it was Buck. I was sure Penny could tell by my frown that there was a problem.

*

Chapter 2

I listened then hung up and sat silently. Penny had finished getting out of her TV persona and back to being my wife. I looked at her. "Trouble?" she asked as her people were finishing up and putting their equipment away.

"The shelter had its first fatality," I replied, feeling upset. "A man hung himself in a bathroom from the shower rod. The police came and the first responders determined it was a suicide, but Joe Lang came to take the body to the morgue and determined otherwise. Looks like there was a murder."

I knew Penny would have loved to razz me about my murder curse, but she knew the shelter was meaningful to me. So she didn't say anything. "Who's taking the lead?" she asked.

"It's in Deacon's jurisdiction so I guess he'll be on the scene. Since we are part owners of the shelter, we need to be there. Shall we go?" I asked while I stood, picking up Willy.

"Who called you?" Penny asked as she followed me out of the room.

"Buck. He was helping Mac with rounds and to check the guards. They found the body. He didn't say much else about it. I guess he figured I'd find out when we got there."

We left the studio and went out to my car. We left Penny's car to be picked up later, and I drove over to the shelter. The building sat in a sparse business section at the west end of Tropicana Road. We had no problems from the surrounding businesses, as most weren't open to the public. I knew in the past, a lot of shelters and half-way houses were chased out of neighborhoods because residents objected to having such organizations so close. We weren't in danger of that. We had our share of trouble, but it never spilled over to the neighboring properties, so they didn't bother us as long as we didn't bother them.

I pulled into the parking lot and saw the ME wagon and two patrol cars. There was a small gathering of the shelter residents watching the proceedings. I saw Buck, Mac and Harold standing with Deacon, they were all talking. Penny and I went over to them.

"Jim, death is not something we need here," Harold said as I came up.

"Death shouldn't be allowed anywhere. What's the deal?"

13

Wiseguy Murders

Deacon nodded his hellos to Penny and me and said, "Buck and Mac found the vic hanging from the shower curtain rod. He was lashed to it by his neck with a rope, no noose, just hanging from the rod. There was no way he could have snapped his neck the way it happens when a person is actually hanged with a noose and dropped. The only way he could have died was by strangulation. Joe Lang examined the body and said there was no petechial hemorrhage of the eyes or around the throat. He used some light to see if he could find any sign of being asphyxiated due to the hanging. He said it looked like the vic was dead before he was strung up. After he gets the body back to the morgue he'll let me know the cause of death."

"Either way, this is not good for the shelter. We need to keep this contained without a lot of nosey press," I said. I turned to Mac, "Be sure to have your guards on high alert tonight. I don't think this will happen again, but just to be sure."

Mac nodded and said he'd go warn his men. He left us and went off. I looked around at the people gathered, watching the commotion. They were all homeless residents and were not expecting all the excitement. They at least had access to showers and a bar of soap, and we managed to get most of them clean clothes so they looked presentable.

Bob Moats

Joe Lang came by to say he would call as soon as he knew something then went off with the black wagon.

I looked to Harold, "What do you know about the victim?"

Harold had a file in hand. He opened it and read, "Name's Martin Scarpo. He lost his job and his family due to excessive drinking. He started to live on the streets after his wife threw him out. I'll contact her to see what she wants to do with the body."

"Be gentle," I said. "She may have thrown him out, but still may have some feelings for him. Or maybe not. Let me know."

"It's still early, I'll go call." Harold went off towards the shelter offices.

Deacon said, "I'm going to have to talk to anyone who knew him. His roommate hasn't turned up, so I'm putting him high on the suspect list. I've got Warren and Williams coming to help with the questioning."

"You can use the dining tables in the community room to question them. I don't think you want to haul all these people into the precinct. Weber may not like that," I said.

"Weber's been away from the precinct for a couple days now. I heard he may be on a vacation," Deacon said with a grin.

"Is there an Elvis convention somewhere?" I said with a laugh. "I still can see him in his Elvis costume at the convention they had at the MGM Grand"

"That's a subject I don't bring up around him. Either way, he's gone for a week, or so they say."

Harold came back, I gave Willy to Penny and she put his leash on to let him do his business. I turned to Harold. "Get hold of the wife?"

"Yeah, she doesn't want anything to do with him. She divorced him two years ago and wants nothing to connect him to her," Harold said.

"Well, he'll have to be buried eventually. See what you can do to take care of that and do a simple burial or cremation."

"Cost less to have him cremated. I've had it done for other homeless before."

"Good, take care of it then." I looked over to Penny standing at the edge of the parking lot waiting for Willy. Deacon asked Harold to help him organize the tenants to be questioned just as Warren arrived with Williams and they joined Deacon.

Buck was standing nearby and taking everything in. "Are we going to investigate this, Chief?"

"I think Deacon will ask for help when he feels the need. Why don't you hang in with him and help out so we know what to expect if he does need us."

Buck grinned and said, "I'll keep him on the straight path to solving the crime." He went off to join Deacon.

Penny came back to me and said, "We need to eat. Why don't we go visit Angelo and have a nice dinner."

I looked at my watch, it was almost four. The day seemed to zip by again. I didn't know if it's a sign of getting older or if the Earth was spinning faster. Either way, the days seemed to move way too fast lately.

"Angelo's sounds good. Maybe Carol is working. We haven't seen much of her lately."

Penny handed Willy to me and said, "Good, let's boogie." She walked off as I wondered what brought the boogie on? My crazy wife, I think I'll keep her.
*

Chapter 3

Penny was humming a tune I didn't recognize while on the way to Angelo's restaurant. I called ahead because I knew Mama Mia was getting more popular and Angelo had to turn people away. I knew he'd find room for us, but I wanted to warn him so he wouldn't move customers around if we got there unannounced. I pulled up to the door to let Penny out, when a young man came to open my door.

"Welcome, Mr. Richards. I'll park your car."

I was a bit surprised. I didn't know Angelo started valet service. I looked around to be sure I wasn't going to have my car stolen. I saw the sign for valet parking and relaxed. I handed him the keys and then warned him about Willy. "Be sure to see he's locked in with the windows down a bit. If he comes up missing, I'll be looking for you," I said with a gruff voice.

He gave me a slightly shocked look and said, "I'll take good care of him." He jumped in the car and drove off. I joined Penny at the entrance and we went in. Angelo was at the front counter and saw us.

"Mr. and Mrs. R, so good to see youse." I noticed he was slipping back to his leg breaker vernacular.

"Angelo, good to see you. How's business?"

"Booming. I have a table ready for youse." He led us into the busy main dining room and over by the fireplace. We sat and I asked, "Is Carol working today?"

"She is, I'll send her out to visit," Angelo said and went off.

Carol came out and sat. "Angelo said to come out and visit. I don't argue with him," she said with a smile. We talked a short while then the waitress came over and took our order.

Angelo came back and asked if he could sit. "Of course, my friend, you don't need to ask. A chair is always waiting for you."

He sat and asked, "How's the shelter doing?"

I hated to bring up the murder but I couldn't keep it from him. I told him about what we found and he kept shaking his head as I spoke.

Wiseguy Murders

"No honor among any types of people. Even the homeless are prime for murder," he said. "Did you find out who the homeless person was?"

"They had his name on a file. Some guy named Martin Scarpo," I said.

Angelo went silent, and had a distressed look on his face. He stood and said, "Excuse me, I have to check on something." He turned and walked quickly away from the table.

I looked at Penny and said, "That was strange. When I said the name, he looked like he swallowed his tongue."

"Maybe someone he knew. Angelo knows a lot of people," Carol said.

"That's probably it. I was surprised that he knew Fred when we brought him here. I guess we'll eventually find out what's up with Angelo."

Our food came and Carol excused herself to go back to the kitchen. Penny and I were enjoying our meal as I looked around the dining room at all the people eating and talking. I noticed at a couple tables there were just men, and they reminded me of the leg breakers Angelo used to help us in our cases. I wondered how many mob figures would come in to eat knowing Angelo was the owner.

About fifteen minutes later, and after we had finished our food, Angelo came back. He sat without asking this time and put his elbows on the table, cradling his head on his fists. He looked concerned.

"Mr. R, what do you know about this guy hanged in the shelter?" he asked.

"Well, from what Harold told us, he was married and lost his job and wife due to excessive drinking. Harold called the wife about taking the body, but she said she divorced him two years ago and wanted nothing to do with him. That's about as much as I know. Why are you interested in him?"

"I think he may be a cousin on my mother's side. My mom has three sisters and it sounds like he's one of the Scarpo family."

I hated to use the term around Angelo but asked, "He may be part of a mob family?"

"No, the Scarpos aren't part of any family. They prefer to stay away from our lifestyle. Although I haven't seen Marty in at least ten years, I don't know what he may have gotten tied up in. I called back home and Mom said last she heard, Marty was married and lived here. So I figure it must be him. Can I go see the body?"

Wiseguy Murders

"I'll call Deacon. I'm sure he won't have a problem with you going to the morgue to identify him. Any thoughts on why he was hung?"

"By the way you described the way he was hung, sounds like a warning. Murder a man, then hang him up to be found. But I don't get where he was hung. Why a homeless shelter and in the bathroom?"

"Something to think about. Can you call around and see if this was mob related?" I asked.

"Yeah. I'll get on it later. When can we see him?"

"I'll call now," I said and pulled out my cell phone. I speed dialed Deacon and explained the situation. He said he was about finished with the questioning and could meet us at the morgue shortly. I thanked him and hung up. "You have time now to go?" I asked Angelo.

"I'll let my people know that I'll be back." He stood and left us. I paid the check and Penny and I went to the front entrance. We waited for Angelo.

He came up a few minutes later and we went out. The valet saw us with his boss and moved quickly to bring my car around. He smiled as he opened my door. "I kept an eye on your dog, sir." I grinned and gave him a good tip.

Bob Moats

We arrived at the county morgue in good time. I saw Deacon at the entrance talking to Joe Lang. We walked up and waited for them to finish.

"Joe, this is my good friend Angelo DeMarko. Angelo, this is the county medical examiner, Joe Lang." They shook hands. Angelo said hello to Deacon.

Joe said, "I was just telling Deacon that the deceased was murdered by something injected into his body. I found the puncture wound, but won't know what he was given until testing is complete. I presume you want to ID the body," he said to Angelo.

The big man nodded, not looking happy. Even though Angelo hadn't seen his cousin in years, family was still family, and important. Joe led us in and to the observation window. He asked us to wait there and went around the other side to pull the body over to the window. He looked to us and I nodded. Joe pulled the cloth back enough to see the man's face.

I could hear Angelo exhale slightly and he said, "It's him." He turned away from the window and we followed him. "I'd like to make arrangements for his burial," Angelo said softly. "I have to call Mom now."

*

Chapter 4

I waved to Joe so he recovered the body and pushed the gurney back to the cold storage.

Angelo stepped aside to use his cell phone. Deacon said, "We questioned as many of the residents at the shelter as we could, no one knew anything. Or they just weren't talking. They're a very guarded people. Not trusting much."

"I can imagine, what with the treatment they've been given," I said. "Angelo said the killing sounded like a warning, but to who and why in the shelter, he didn't know. How long had Scarpo been one of the residents, I wonder?"

Deacon had the folder that Harold had on the man. He opened it and read, "It says that Scarpo came with the original group from the tunnels to stay at the shelter when it opened."

"So, he lived there about a month. If he came with the rest of the people, someone had to have known him," I said.

"We talked to a couple of men who knew of him, but they said he was very tight-lipped about his life. He never spoke much to anyone. One man said he would go out during the day and not come back until evening. Then he would go into his little section of the tunnel where he camped. No one knew what he was doing when he was out."

"I'm sure no one cared what he was doing. They had enough problems of their own to have to worry about someone else," I said.

"That's the impression I got. These people are not very social."

Angelo came back to us and said, "Mom's going to call her sister and break the news. Tragic. I'd like to be informed of any progress you make on this," he said to Deacon.

Deacon said he would inform him. I presumed that Deacon didn't want the mob to get involved in the case, but giving out a little info couldn't hurt.

Angelo continued to tell Deacon, "Gino said he could have some of his people help find the killer, if you need them."

"You tell your step-father I appreciate that, I'll let you know." I knew Deacon didn't want any mob involvement, but when the capo of a mob family

Wiseguy Murders

in New York offers to have his people in on the case, you don't just say no. Deacon was being subtle.

"There's not much more you can do here, so I'll drive you back to the restaurant," I told Angelo. Penny and I took Angelo out to the car after saying goodbye to Deacon and Joe.

He was quiet on the way back. Then he broke the silence. "I used to play with Marty when we were kids, we would play cops and robbers, of course. I was always the robber, Marty was always the cop. He took the game seriously. We got older and I started getting more involved in my real father's business. First I was a runner for his numbers, Marty didn't want anything to do with it, and I never bothered him about it." Angelo went silent again. I didn't push him. "Marty was a popular kid, as a teen he had a number of girlfriends. I envied him, I wasn't very good looking, like he was." He was quiet again. "Rest in peace, Marty," he finally said, just before we got back to his restaurant.

I pulled up to the valet parking of the building and waved the man off. Angelo just sat a few moments, not saying anything. When he spoke, his voice was somber, "You know, we have friends and relatives we take for granted. I've always tried to be good to my friends and have respect for my family. I'm not happy about this. Marty was family." That's all he said and then got out of the car.

We watched him go into the restaurant and Penny looked at me, "Shouldn't we do something for him?"

"Just let him grieve, I don't know what more we can do. I'll check on him later and see how he's holding up. I just hope he takes it easy. He sounded like he may do something about it. I hope he stays cool."

We drove away from Angelo's and went to the office. Fred was out back with his dog Henry. He came over to us as we exited the car. "I heard about the death at the shelter, do you know what happened?" he asked.

"Put the dogs in the dog run and come inside. I need to talk to you," I said and went to the back door. Penny put Willy in the pen with Henry and she came in with Fred. I was in my office when they caught up to me.

"Fred, sit down. I need to ask you a few questions." Fred sat and Penny said she was going up to see Lacey.

"What do you want to ask me?" Fred said.

"Did you ever know a man by the name Martin Scarpo?"

"Sure, he's lived in the tunnels. Not a very friendly guy, I figured he had a rough past. Was he the man killed at the shelter?"

"How'd you know about it?"

"Buck came in about an hour ago and told us. Then he said he was going back to the shelter to see what more he could find out."

"Well, I found out some new information. It seems that Martin Scarpo was Angelo's cousin. I just got back from taking Angelo to identify the body. He's not very happy. Do you think he may try something?"

"Angelo has a big sense of attachment to his family, no matter who. It's been years that I haven't been in touch with him, until recently. I don't know what he may do. I suppose there's nothing pointing to the killer yet?"

"No, it's all being investigated so far. I'm hoping CSI will come up with something to point to a perp, and quickly, before things get complicated. Angelo talked to his mother back in New York and Gino has offered to help find the killer."

"Not good for the family to get involved. Could be bad for the police," Fred said.

"Could be bad for a lot of people. Especially if this was some kind of hit on Scarpo. The coroner said he was murdered before he was hung. Angelo said the hanging was some kind of warning, but to who?"

"You can wrack your brain trying to come up with theories, or just wait and see if something more happens," Fred said. I thought he was right. "If this was a warning, there will be some after effect."

"True, I guess we wait. Thanks for your input. It helps." I stood and said, "Let's go see what the girls are plotting up front."

We left my office and went up the hallway to the front. There was no one in the lobby, I went to the outer lobby and found Penny, Lacey and Tracey all standing at the counter talking. They shut up when Fred and I came out.

"What's going on?" I asked.

Penny said, "Nothing. We're just talking about fashions. Clothes, make-up and things feminine. You wouldn't understand that."

"I'm not totally out of the loop. I pay attention to your fashions and make-up. What's so special?"

Penny smiled and looked at Tracey, then said, "We were talking about giving Tracey a make-over."

*

Chapter 5

After hearing that, I tried not to laugh. Tracey was young and she had a plain beauty about her. She never wore make-up or wore fancy clothes. I knew she wasn't well off, and the salary she made here was what she had to live on. I presumed clothes were not high on her list to buy.

"I think that's a great idea," I said and looked at Penny. "You can take her to get a whole new wardrobe too, on the firm. We have to maintain an image here and Tracey is the first person people see when they come in. Buy her what she needs."

Penny gave me a wink and a smile. "We'll do that today, if we can take off?"

"Sure, I can put one of Buck's guards up front to handle the inflow of clients. Go have a good time."

I gave her the company credit card and went back into the offices followed by Fred.

"I could watch the front while they're gone," Fred offered. "I've watched Lacey do it enough to know how it works."

"Perfect. You're hired. Hold my calls as I'll be meditating in my office."

"Lacey says that's when you take a nap," he said with a grin.

I was holding the laugh and said, "I call it meditating." I left him at the counter and went to my office. I figured I could sit back in my chair and catch a couple nods of sleep.

About an hour later, Buck came into my office and plopped down on a chair. I gathered my head together from the sleep and looked at him. "What?"

"Those people don't trust much do they?" he said.

"The residents? No, most of them don't. Which is something Harold and I talked about. Try to get them to open up about their lives so they can get on with their lives."

Wiseguy Murders

"You know some of them have mental problems."

"That's what our on-site counselors are for. To try and get them into a program to get help. I know we can't help everyone, but we can try. Have you heard about Angelo?"

"No, what?"

"That dead man you found is Angelo's cousin. Penny and I went to eat and I mentioned the name of the deceased and Angelo recognized him. I took him to the morgue and Angelo identified Scarpo as his cousin."

"Well, he must not be happy."

"No, unfortunately, he's not happy. I hope he doesn't do something crazy to find the killer."

"Maybe the police should just let it go and let the mob find him. Would save a lot of police manpower," Buck said with a grin.

"It would, and I sort of agree, but we have to maintain the balance of justice in the proper way."

"I don't see much justice in this crappy world," he said.

"I agree. So what are you going to do now?"

"I'm going back to the shelter to keep trying to get them to talk. They had to know something," he said and stood. "Give my condolences to Angelo. I have to go to my office and get something. See you later." He walked out as quickly as he came in.

I stood and went out to find Fred at Lacey's desk. Willy and Henry were sleeping on the couch in the waiting area. "I see they finally wore themselves out."

"I brought them in about a half hour ago. They went right for the couch when I put them down. You got a call from a man just as Buck went into your office. I didn't want to interrupt and he said just to give you a message."

Fred handed me the slip of paper with a name and number. "He said to call him at your convenience."

"Thanks Fred." I looked at the paper then went back into my office. I sat and picked up my desk phone and dialed the number. After a few rings, a voice said, "Hello."

"I'm Jim Richards and I was told someone wanted to talk to me," I said to the phone.

"That was me. Thank you for calling back. I was recommended to your firm by a friend who shall remain nameless. She's used your service before," he said.

"Okay, I'm not going to ask. But what is it you need?"

"I have a problem that I don't want anyone to know about, publically I mean."

"We are discrete. You can be certain that no one else will know what we are investigating. Please continue or would you rather come in to talk?" I offered.

He was quiet for a moment. "I can be there in ten minutes, thank you."

"What's your name, please?" He told me Jason Frisard. "I'll wait for you, Mr. Frisard," I said and hung up. I stood and went to Lynn's office. She was at her desk reading something. She looked up and smiled.

"Hey, Jim. What's up?" she asked.

"I have a possible client coming in, but I'm on a case involving a murder at the shelter."

"Buck told us about that," she said sympathetically.

"But he didn't know then that the victim was a cousin of Angelo's. I want to be around to see Angelo doesn't do anything crazy."

"Good luck with that. Do you know what this possible client wants?"

"Compete anonymity. He said we were recommended by a person we helped previously. We won't know what he wants until he gets here. I hope you can help him."

"Just what I need, a surprise. When is he going to be here?"

"Any moment. I think if we go to the lobby, we'll find him waiting," I assumed.

She smiled and stood. We went up front and found a small man in the lobby. I mean as in a little person. As I knew it, it wasn't proper to call them midgets or dwarfs, as they'd been referred to in the past, they wanted to be known as little people. That was fine with me. But the way I saw it, we were all just people.

"Are you Jason Frisard?" I asked, approaching him with my hand extended.

"I am, thank you for seeing me on such short notice," he said, shaking my hand.

Wiseguy Murders

"This is my associate, Lynn DeAngelo, she will be helping you, if that's acceptable to you."

"I don't care who investigates, just as long as the job gets done," he said as he and Lynn shook hands.

"Good, follow us please." I turned to the glass door and opened it, allowing the diminutive man to enter. Lynn smiled at me and we followed. I pointed him to Lynn's office door and we went there.

Lynn asked him to have a seat and he climbed up with no effort at all. I sat on the end of the desk away from them and waited. Lynn asked, "What is it you need of us, Mr. Frisard?"

"Please, call me Jason. I think my wife is cheating on me and I need proof," he said quietly.

I gritted my teeth, a spousal surveillance case. We knew they meant money, but none of us liked working them. Especially when we were required to go to testify in court. I still had nightmares about shyster lawyer Alphonse Grisler and the case I had to testify on.

"Why do you feel your wife is cheating on you?" Lynn asked.

"Text messages on her phone that she didn't erase. Not very clever of her. I managed to forward them to my computer," he said, and opened a file he was carrying. He removed a couple pieces of paper and handed them to Lynn.

She read them and said, "Well, I'd say these could be construed as evidence in spouse cheating. What more do you need?"

"Photos," he said, "and I want to know who this man is that she's seeing. I work at the Harmon Theatre in one of the shows along with my wife. There are a number of men who work there and I feel it's one of them."

"What show is that?" I asked, having been to the Harmon a few times.

"It's a freak and geek show. My wife does body piercings and I help a magician with sawing a man in half. I'm the top half," he said with a grin.

*

Chapter 6

Now I knew where I had seen this man. I remembered the show and his wife sticking herself with long needles through her body. It made me shiver.

Lynn smiled and said, "Well, I haven't seen the show, but I'm sure I will soon. I need to see your wife so I can get a fix on her. Can you give me a list of places she goes so I can keep track of her?" Lynn handed the man a pad of paper and a pencil. He put the pad on his lap and started to write.

I stood and quietly told Lynn that I was going to check on my case. She smiled and I left the room. I went through to the lobby to get to my office but found Penny, Lacey and Tracey at the counter. It was covered with bags, packages, and boxes and they were all excited. I slipped around them and made a break to my office before they noticed me. Luckily, they were all wrapped up in the purchases to stop me.

I went to my desk and picked up the phone. I called Buck. He came on after two rings. "Hey, Buck. Where are you?"

"I'm at the shelter, talking to people. I think I'm making head way," he replied.

"I'll be out shortly. Is Deacon around?" I asked.

"He's with Harold and they've been busy talking," he responded.

"Okay, I'll be there in a short while. Later." I hung up and stood. I peeked out my door to see if the women were in the hallway. The only person I saw was Fred, coming my way. "You don't want to see me, do you?"

"No, the women are busy glamming up Tracey. I had to get away before I needed a testosterone shot," he said with a grin.

I had to laugh at that. Fred was cleverer than he let on. I think he had a high IQ, but I wasn't going to embarrass him by asking.

"Well, you haven't seen me. No, tell them I had to go to the shelter to investigate the murder. Hold down the fort and don't let the women turn the lobby into a fashion show."

He grinned and said he would cover for me. I knew that both Earl and Trapper were out on cases, I checked earlier, so I slipped out the back door to my car.

Wiseguy Murders

I arrived at the shelter about ten minutes later and parked next to Buck's car. I went into the community room and found the residents eating. At the far end of the room were Buck, Deacon and Harold standing at a table talking. I approached and they saw me.

"About time you started to get in on this case," Deacon said with a grin.

"Well, I knew you couldn't handle it, so here I am," I replied.

"Now, what's this about the victim being Angelo's cousin?" Harold asked.

"All I know is, I told him the name of our victim and he went pale. For Angelo, that's a lot. He checked and said it could be his cousin, then we met with Deacon at the morgue where Angelo identified the body. I hope Angelo lets us investigate the case and doesn't get involved."

Deacon was looking past me towards the entrance of the community room. He said, "You may have spoken too soon." He nodded in the direction behind me and I turned. I saw Angelo come in with two large men behind him. One looked like the bodyguard Angelo sent to watch over Harold when he was being threatened. We met Angelo halfway across the room and I said, "Angelo, what can we do for you, my friend?"

"Mr. R, I just wanted to see the room where Marty bought it," he said and looked at Deacon. "If that's all right with LVPD?"

Deacon smiled, not wanting to rile the man, he said, "I'll personally take you there. Is there something you're looking for in particular?"

"I'll know if I see it," he said quietly.

Deacon said, "Okay, follow me." He turned to the door as we all followed.

The one big man I thought I knew looked back and said, "Good to see you again, Mr. Richards. Angelo gave me a job."

It was Mario, the man who helped get the hitman ring taken down during the Santa case. "I'm glad Mario. Good to see you're still alive."

He gave me a huge grin and winked. "I got good people to work for now. They take care of me."

I didn't want to ask just who was taking care of him, I presumed it was Angelo. I was still getting the feeling that Angelo was getting his own little family set up here. Would I have to start calling him 'don' Angelo DeMarko now? Kissing his ring? He held himself up well enough to be a capo, and he had the looks to frighten anyone. I was glad to be on his favorite list.

We came around to the door of the room where Buck and Mac found the body. Deacon took down the yellow tape from one side of the door and opened it. We went in and Angelo asked where they found the body. Deacon asked us to wait in the main room and took Angelo to the bathroom. Deacon let Angelo go in first and the man stood in the middle of the room looking around. Deacon stood in the doorway while Angelo studied the room. We stood just outside watching them. Angelo reached for the door and pulled it in a little so he could see the back of the door, after Deacon came further into the room. He examined the door and smiled.

Angelo opened it back up slightly so Deacon could see the back of the door and said, "This was a mob hit. See this mark? It's a symbol of warning to someone. I don't know who, but this person is marked for a vendetta. I assume my cousin was in the wrong place since he's never been associated with a family. Who else was staying in this room?"

"There was another man staying in here, but we haven't located him yet." Deacon looked to Harold, "Who was the other man living here?"

Harold said to hold on and went to the front entrance and looked at the plaque on the door. He read the name aloud, "Sal Rasman."

I was watching Angelo and his face turned serious, his frown lines were getting deep. He looked at Deacon, "Just because you is a friend of Mr. R, I'll share this with you. Sal Rasman was a lowlife soldier in a former mob family here in Vegas. They disbanded years ago and the capo of that family left with many enemies. His boss's name was Rico Romanny. I'm sure your OCU would have a file on him. If not, the FBI will. Romanny went into hiding and hasn't been seen in all these years. I'd say someone was looking for him."

"Any idea why?" Deacon asked.

"Seems Romanny left with millions of dollars in mob funds. Could be a reason why someone wants him. He's a dead man if they find him and the money."

*

Chapter 7

Deacon looked out to us standing in the room. "Well, we have motive now, thanks to Angelo. Now we need to locate this Rasman and find out what he knows."

Harold spoke up, "He may have gone back into the tunnels to hide. I don't know if these gangsters would find him in there."

I saw Angelo smile at the gangster reference. "I'm sure if they want him, they'll go all through the tunnels to find him." He left the bathroom followed by Deacon. "I'd like to talk to him myself. I think someone came here for Rasman and found my cousin. He wouldn't have known anything, but they assumed he did from his association with Rasman. They left Rasman a message, and he ran."

"Doesn't make sense to warn him that they're after him," Deacon said. "If they wanted him, they could have waited until he came back."

"These people think on a different level. They survive through intimidation and aren't so clever. They know he's scared to death now and he'll screw up. Possibly run to Romanny and get him stirred up. They'd kill two birds with one stone."

"Where would a former mob boss hide out in Vegas? He started here, right. People know him. Why not leave and go far away?" I asked.

Angelo said, "I'm sure he still has people working for him, they could be protecting him from the public. He could hole up in some fancy digs, like an expensive home in the valley, and let others go out to do his dirty work. Rasman was expendable and became an outsider. I'm surprised they didn't bump him off."

"Maybe his hiding in the tunnels under Vegas helped to keep him alive," Harold said.

Deacon said, "I can run a check on expensive property around Vegas to see if this Romanny has a deed somewhere."

"It wouldn't be in his name, for sure," I said.

"Try Ronald Manny. I heard he used that name on his dirty business ventures," Angelo offered.

"Thanks, I'll try that." We all went out of the room.

Wiseguy Murders

We were standing in the parking area of the building and I asked, "Angelo, are you planning on doing something about this yourself?"

"No, Mr. R, I'm a businessman now with my restaurant, and I don't want to dirty my hands with this. I know you and the police can take care of business." He grinned and signaled to his men to leave.

When the three men were out of earshot, Buck said, "I like Angelo, but why do I think this isn't over for him?"

"You could be right, Buck. Time will tell," I replied.

"I just hope nothing bad goes down. Angelo has worked hard to become a leading businessman in the restaurant community," Deacon said. "Well, shall we go back and see if we can find anything out about Rasman from the former tunnel dwellers?"

We all went back to the community room. The lunch crowd had finished and left the room nearly empty, save for the kitchen staff. Deacon asked Harold if he could find the people who came in the same group from the tunnels with Rasman. Harold said he would go get the files for the people and also dig out the photo of him.

Bob Moats

When we opened the shelter, we made it mandatory that all residents be photographed for identification purposes. That way we had ID on our people. And Rasman could be identified now.

"I'll have Rasman run through the system to see what we have on him. I'll also talk to OCU about Romanny. This should be interesting, we haven't had a good mob war in a long while."

"I just hope Angelo keeps his head down," I said.

We sat at the table where we would ask questions of the residents again. Harold came back and had run off copies of Rasman's photo and gave one to each of us. He went out and brought back the residents who lived closest to Rasman and Angelo's cousin.

He brought in four men and Harold had them sit on chairs near us. He brought over one man to start.

"Name?" Deacon asked the man after he sat across from us.

"Leo Wicher," the man said quietly.

"Leo, did you know this man?" Deacon asked, showing him the photo. Leo leaned forward and squinted at the picture. He studied it, then sat back.

"I've seen him, yeah. Didn't know him though. Did he kill Marty?"

"You knew Marty Scarpo?"

"Sure, everyone liked Marty. It was a shock to hear he was killed."

"This man in the photo is wanted by us for questioning in Marty's murder. Were Marty and the man in this picture friends?"

"I don't think so, they just shared a room. Most of us didn't have much say in who we lived with. You should change that."

I made mental note to work with Harold on arranging the residents a little better.

Deacon had one more question, "If you know anything that might help us find him, you'll let us know?"

"I'll ask around, we all watch each other. It's too bad we didn't watch Marty better," Leo said. "May I go now?"

Deacon looked to me and I just shrugged. "Sure, go see if you and your friends can figure out where this man is at. His name is Sal Rasman."

When Deacon mentioned the name, I could see a reaction on Leo's face. "Excuse me, Leo. You seemed to remember the name, but not the face. Why?"

Leo sat thinking, "I may have heard the name thrown around by some people who visited us the other day."

"What people, and where did they come from?" Harold asked.

"There were two men who came to us in the parking lot while we played basketball. They asked if we knew anyone by that name. None of us did and they left."

"Did they have a car that you saw?" Deacon asked.

"No, we were busy shooting hoops."

"Think you could identify any of the men if we showed you pictures?"

"I have a pretty good memory, I think I could spot them. Sure."

"Great, just hang in with us and I'll have one of my men take you to show you some photos. Is that good for you?"

"Yeah, I guess. What's in it for me?" he asked.

Ah, yes. Nothing comes for free, I thought.

"How about extra TV privileges, Leo," Harold offered.

The man smiled at that. "I like that, sure. When do I go to see the pictures?"

"As soon as my man gets here. Go over to those chairs and wait," Deacon said, pointing to chairs behind us. He pulled out his cell phone and I heard him talking to Detective Warren. He hung up and looked at us.

"I'll have Warren take him to OCU and have him look through the mob member books to see if he can find them. This may work yet."

We talked to a few more people, but nothing as good as Leo gave us came up. Warren came in and Deacon took him to Leo, introduced them, and then the two men left.

"Okay, there's not much more we can do here. I'll go check on Romanny in the system and see if he's still hanging around. But, if the mob can't find him, I'm sure we won't."

*

Chapter 8

I didn't have anything to check. Warren had Leo looking at mug shots of mob figures to see if he could identify the men who inquired about Rasman. Maybe they were involved in the murder of Angelo's cousin. Deacon was going to talk to Organized Crime Unit to see if they had anything on Romanny, the former mob boss, now in hiding. Me, I had nothing.

Sometimes it's good to have nothing to take up my time. I went back to the office to see if the women had transformed Tracey into a goddess. I went in the back door of the building and saw Willy standing down the other end of the hallway. He saw me and came rushing down to me. He looked funny, his fur flying all over the place. I bent down to pick him up and he was trying to wash me with his tongue. I didn't mind doggy kisses, as long as he kept away from my face.

Wiseguy Murders

I heard the door open and out came Penny. She probably saw me on the security camera over the back door that showed on Lacey's monitor on her desk.

"Hey sweetie, did you solve the case yet?" she asked.

"No, but we found some interesting facts. I'll tell you in my office," I said and went past her to my door and in. She followed.

"So, have you made Tracey into a glamor queen?" I asked.

"No, but we did make her to look like an attractive young woman. She's actually cute without make-up, but a girl has to accent her assets," Penny said and sat on my lap.

She put her arms around me and licked my ear. "Stop that. Don't start something we can't finish here."

"Spoilsport," she said and stood. She sat in my client chair and said, "Tell me about the mob hit."

I went over the morning and told her everything I knew. She sat nodding as I talked.

Tracey came to the door and I was shocked. She looked adorable. "What do you need, Tracey?"

"Lacey sent me to you to say there's a man in the lobby who wants to talk to you," she said and turned to go. I told her to wait.

"Tracey, you look very nice. I'm impressed," I said with a grin.

She gave me a blushing smile and went off.

"I didn't embarrass her, did I?" I asked Penny.

"No, you just made her day," she responded.

We left my office and walked out to the lobby. There was a rather good looking young man waiting for me. I hoped Penny didn't start drooling.

"May I help you?" I asked.

"I hope so, you need to prevent a murder," he replied.

I was stunned by his comment. "Well, I guess we need to get to work. Follow me please." I led him back to my office and asked him to sit. "You are?"

"Lance Hartwell."

"Now what makes you think someone is going to be murdered, and who is it?"

"I think I may be murdered. By my girlfriend's husband."

I cringed hearing that. "Okay, explain."

"My girlfriend is keeping tabs on her husband and she knows he came here to hire someone to follow her."

I thought of the little person.

"If he finds out it's me, he'll murder me. The man is crazy and not below killing."

I had an image of Jason Frisard shooting this man in the knees. Not a nice image, but I couldn't help it.

"I presume you're talking about Frisard. His wife is keeping tabs on him?"

"Yes, she hired a cheap P.I. and he saw her husband come here. What else would he come here for? Did he hire you?"

"Not me. One of my associates. I really shouldn't be talking about this. Our client wanted his information to remain confidential. This could be a conflict of interest. If my associate identifies you, we can't guarantee to protect you. Why don't you just get out of the situation before my associate finds you? Then we can say we couldn't find out who the other man was."

He thought about that. "I suppose it could work. I hope Alicia can agree to it. It was bad enough that she hired the P.I. to follow him. She doesn't trust the man. I don't either. I've worked with him in the show and I know he has a terrible temper. The last man who was seeing his wife strangely disappeared."

"She's seen other men? I hate to say it, but this woman isn't interested in just you. Why do you bother?"

"The woman is phenomenal. In addition to body piercings, she's a contortionist. Have you ever had sex with a contortionist?"

I thought about Penny, but she wasn't that limber. "I can understand the enjoyment of sex, but if it's with someone who is married, it can cause problems. You need to get on and find someone else. You're a good looking guy, I'm sure you could have any woman you want."

"I guess you're right. My life is worth more than a roll in bed. I'll take a vacation from the show, just until things cool down."

"Good idea. I can't tell my associate about this, which would be conflicting to what he wanted us to do. Just stay away for a while."

"If I leave her, she'll latch on to another man. I guess it's better than me," he said with a frown. "Do I owe you anything for the advice?"

"No, this is a freebie. Just save yourself and get lost," I said, then stood. "What was the name of the other man who disappeared after being with her?"

"Harry Seguro, he was the sword swallower. We haven't seen him in a couple months."

"Thanks, go and be safe." I led him back to the lobby and he thanked me. He went out and I turned to Lacey at her desk.

"Is he now a client?" she asked.

"No, I don't think we can help him. He needs to work this out himself." I said and turned to Penny standing with Willy. "Feel like eating at Angelo's?"

"You are such a smooth talker," she said.

I told Lacey we'd be out. She made no snide remark, so I left quickly, followed by Penny.

We arrived at Angelo's restaurant and he was more than happy to see us. "Mr. and Mrs. R, good to see you. In for dinner?"

"Yes, my friend, how are you feeling?" I asked.

He paused, thinking. Then said, "I'm good. I know you and the police will track down the killers. Justice will be served."

I hoped that justice better be served, or mob justice would take over. "So, do you have a table open?" I asked looking into the busy dining area.

"Nope, but I can set you two up in the banquet room, if you don't mind?"

"No, that will be nice and quiet. Lead the way," I said and we followed him through a door to the large room. It was quiet and dark. Angelo turned on a wall sconce over a table by the door, it was romantic. We sat and he said, "Now that we are out of the general public's hearing, I have something to tell you. You can find Rico Romanny out just past Summerlin." He handed me a piece of paper, which I opened and found an address.

*

Chapter 9

I folded the paper back up. "I won't ask where you got this, but I appreciate you giving it to me."

"You mean, gave it to you instead of going out to chase him myself," Angelo said with a big grin.

"That too. I'll see that Deacon gets this as soon as possible. Now, we need to eat."

"I'll have your server to you posthaste," he said, then went out the door.

"Posthaste? Angelo is really working on his vocabulary," I said.

"He's a well-respected businessman now, he needs to sound like one," Penny added.

"Very true," I said as I pulled out my cell phone. I speed dialed Deacon. I put the phone on speaker and waited. He came on after two rings.

"Jim, I was just going to call you. I talked to OCU and they lost track of Romanny about two years ago. The man is hiding very well. Even from the feds, I called them. What's up?"

"Romanny may hide from the law, but he can't hide from Angelo. I got an address if you want it."

"Are you serious? Is Angelo going to take on Romanny?" Deacon sounded excited.

"No, he wants us to take the man. Although it's not Romanny who had Angelo's cousin murdered. There's another force at work here. Has Warren called to let us know if Leo recognized any photos?"

"Leo went through all the mob related mug shots, now they have him going through the regular criminal books. I'm hoping they find at least one face. What's the address?"

I took out the paper again and opened it. I read the address and said, "He lives so close to Vegas, it's surprising no one found him."

"He's hiding behind his soldiers and lieutenants. They take care of the daily grind and he sits back and enjoys the weather. I'm not sharing this with OCU yet. I don't want them blundering into the hornets' nest yet. I'll put a car on watch out at his property."

Wiseguy Murders

"Be careful that Romanny's men don't spot them. They won't know if it's the cops or another gang."

"True, I can have surveillance cameras installed nearby the property to watch. Just to be safe."

"That sounds good," I said as our waitress came in. "Got to go, we have to order our food now." I hung up on him before the waitress could hear our conversation.

She was pleasant and took our orders then said she'd be back with our drinks. I reached out to Penny's hand on the table and held it. She gave me a smile and said, "Think we could get a quick one in before the food comes back?" Then she laughed. I looked around at the empty room and laughed also.

Angelo came back in after we finished our meal. I had already paid the girl, so Angelo couldn't give us another free meal. I appreciated it, but he needed to be more businesslike.

"So, how was the food?" he asked.

"Excellent as always," I replied.

"Good, now you know where Romanny is, see if you can find out who wants the man and why. I know he skipped out with millions of dollars of mob funds, which could be the reason. But I'm sure you'll find that out."

"I hope we do. While we were eating, I was formulating a plan and I may need you to help. Think Romanny would be friendly enough to see you in person?"

Angelo grinned and said, "I've never met the man, but his family and my father's family were on good terms back in the day. He might be willing to see me, along with a good friend of mine, I'm sure. I think I know where you're going with this. When?"

"I'm not sure yet. I have to talk to Deacon and work it out," I said.

"No wire, the man would be real pissed if we went in wired."

"I'm not suicidal. It would be just a fact finding visit. See if he may know who killed your cousin. He may wonder how you found him."

"I go through approved mob channels. We have a network that the feds and the law don't know about. If there's a wiseguy to be found, we can find him."

"Even the ones who murdered your cousin?" I asked.

Wiseguy Murders

"Those men work outside the network, I'm sure they are freelancers hired by someone wanting to find Romanny. Be sure Deacon keeps that address safe. Even the police have corrupt cops in their ranks."

"I'll warn him. Thank you for the info and the great meal," I said and looked at Penny. "Shall we go rescue Willy and go home?"

"Yep, I'm worn out," she replied and stood after Angelo pulled her chair out. "Thank you, kind sir," she told him.

"You two are always welcome. Enjoy your evening." He smiled and went out as we followed him. Penny and I went to the front door and to the valet. By now, the men working valet knew my car and knew to keep an eye on Willy.

We were on our way home when my cell phone buzzed. It was Buck. I pulled into our drive and put the phone on speaker. "Hey, buddy, what's up?"

"We had another visit by the men asking about Rasman. They came into the parking lot where a few men were shooting hoops and started questioning them. One of the residents came in to tell me about it, but by the time I got out there, they were gone. We may have gotten them on our security cameras this time. I'll pull the file and call Deacon."

"Thanks Buck, keep me informed." I hung up.

"I didn't know you had security cameras," Penny said.

"Something we kept talking about. I had Mac put some temporary ones in the front parking and around the back this morning. I'm having him and Buck install permanent ones soon," I said, and got out of the car.

I took Willy for a run and dump, then went into the house. Penny was already on the couch in the living room in front of the TV, with our beer and chips. I loved this woman.

We watched TV for a while, then went to bed. I really hoped I wasn't going to get any phone calls in the night.

Penny snuggled up to me and whispered in my ear, "Do you still love me?"

I smiled, and said, "As long as you keep me in beer and chips, I do."

She started laughing and rolled away. I pulled her back and said, "I love you just as much today as the day we met. I love you more than life itself. I love you more than a new car. I love you more…"

Wiseguy Murders

She said to shut up, then she kissed me and we cuddled.

Of course, if anything could go wrong, it would be at four in the morning. My cell phone buzzed and I almost wished I had shut it off in my sleep again. "This better be real good," I said as I answered, my eyes too blurry to see the caller ID.

It was Buck again. "I know you hate to be woken up so early, but we had another murder."

*

Chapter 10

I'm used to being awakened early to be told someone was dead. It was the story of my life. "Who and how?" I asked Buck.

"Don't know and don't know. Sorry, that's all I got until Deacon and Joe Lang get here. I already called them. Then you." Buck said.

"Where's the body at?" I asked quietly, as I sat up on the bed.

"Next to the ice machine at the end of the building. Just propped up against the building, sitting though. They didn't even bother to close his eyes. Spooky," he said.

"Why are you there so early?"

"I've been here all night. I wanted to hang around to see if those mob men came back. Mac and I have been patrolling the area with the guards. It had to be a dump, we've been around enough to see a murder being committed. So they had to slip in and drop the body off."

Wiseguy Murders

"Okay, I'll be there shortly. Talk later." I hung up and got dressed. I bypassed my morning routine in the bathroom and left a note for Penny who was still sound asleep. I was on the road in seven minutes after I hung up.

I pulled into the lot and saw Deacon's car and the coroner's van. They moved quicker than I did. I went down to the end of the building where everyone was gathering.

"Jim, you got out of bed to join us, how nice," Deacon said with a smirk.

"Shut up. I haven't had breakfast yet, so I'm cranky. What's the deal?"

"Well, someone came from over there," he said, pointing to a road by the building, "and dropped him here."

"How did they get over the fence?" I asked, wondering about how the six foot fence around the building could have been breached.

Deacon yelled to an officer by the fence to show the opening. The officer went by an upright post and pulled the chain link fence back. "It had to be cut another day. Would have taken too long to do that tonight and then drop a body off. Someone planned this early on."

"This is another warning, I feel," Buck said.

"I agree. To go through all this trouble, it means something. Anything on the vic?" I asked.

"No ID on the body. I'll have Warren take prints and see if he's in the system. Harold said he wasn't a resident."

"Are these people trying to scare the residents into giving the location of Rasman?" I asked.

"Only thing I can figure," Deacon said. "If they want to find Rasman, they figure someone must know where he is. So they think if they scare these people, someone will talk."

"How did Leo do scanning the mug books?" I asked.

"Came up with nothing. For a guy who says he has a good memory, he bailed out on us."

"Or, this criminal isn't in your system. Could be someone brought in from outside. I think you mentioned that," I said.

"I did and I still think it's true. I'll have Leo work with a sketch artist today, see if we can pick him up on facial recognition in the national database," Deacon said.

Wiseguy Murders

I turned to Harold and said, "Gather all the residents in the community room."

"Everyone?"

"Yes, all of them, together, now. While they are still groggy from sleep," I said.

"Okay, I'll see what I can do. I'll need some of the guards to help get them moving," Harold said.

Buck said, "No problem, Mac and I will get them to you for instructions." Buck and Mac went off as did Harold.

"What do you have on your devious little mind?" Deacon asked.

"Shake some people up. Maybe someone will talk."

"Okay, if it works. My people have no clue where he could be. They did ask around the tunnels and no one is talking. For all we know, Rasman left the area and is probably in Arizona enjoying the heat."

"Like it's not hot enough here. If I were him, I'd go to the coast, LA or Frisco."

"Sure, make it hard to find him." Deacon frowned.

"Excuse me, but why are we even worrying about Rasman? We now know where Romanny is living, we don't need Rasman."

Deacon was quiet on that. "I guess we don't need him. So what are you going to do with all the residents?"

"We need Rasman to find out why everyone is looking for him. We still don't know if it's even about Romanny. That was just a theory. As soon as Angelo and I go talk to the man, we may learn something."

"Yeah, how to end up in cement boots." Deacon smiled.

"We're too far from water. I'd be concerned about a shallow grave in the desert."

"For all we know, that could be where Rasman is."

"Let's assume he's still alive. Otherwise, the people who want him wouldn't be dropping bodies here and there."

Harold came back out and said the guards had rounded up everyone. Most were already in the community room.

Wiseguy Murders

"Thanks Harold," I told him. I said to Deacon, "Shall we go?"

"Lead the way. This is your show." Deacon laughed and went ahead of me.

I followed him into the room and studied the occupants already there. Most were in bed clothes, robes and some came in their underwear. They all looked tired, the way I felt. Deacon and I stood on the side watching them get settled into the seats. I saw Buck, Mac and Harold come in and over to us.

"That should be all," Buck said. "I got the guards looking for stragglers, but I'm sure we got ninety-eight percent of them."

"Okay, I'll start." I went to the head of the room and waited for the men to quiet down. I didn't figure they would, all rumbling about being pulled out of bed. I knew how they felt. I took my Glock out of its holster and used the butt to bang on a table. It was loud enough to make everyone look towards me. A few men saw the gun and gave me surprised look. I holstered it again and stood as tall as I could.

"Listen up, I'll make this quick and then everyone can go back to bed. This morning we found a body in the back of the building by the ice machine. I'm going to say this is getting dangerous. Two murders in less than a week, not good. Now, the reason we figure these men are dropping bodies, is because they are looking for Sal Rasman. We have one person who is helping to identify the men looking for Rasman. But we need to find Rasman to find out what this is all about. We will guarantee Rasman's safety away from these men, but we don't know where to find him. Someone here in this room must know where he is." I paused to let it sink in. "I'm going to offer five hundred dollars to the first person who can give us a verified location of Rasman. You can come to us after I turn everyone loose. You are saving a life by telling us where he is. All right, go back to your rooms. I'll be in the main office along with my friends. I hope to get an answer. Now go!"

*

Chapter 11

I turned to my friends and nodded. I headed to the main office, followed by Deacon and Harold. Harold went ahead and unlocked the door, as two men approached us.

I turned to them and said, "I hope you have news for me."

They started arguing about who was there first. I told them to stop talking and get inside. Deacon smiled and said, "Hope you can handle this."

I went to the men, "You first, talk to me," I said pointing to one of them.

"I know where Rasman is. I'm first, so I want the money," he said.

I looked to Deacon, "Take this gentleman into the office there and take his statement. I'll deal with this man."

Deacon went off and I took the remaining man to the desk in the front of the outer office. "Sit, and write down where you know Rasman to be." I handed him a pad of paper and pencil. He wrote for a few minutes then handed the pad back.

I looked at the information he wrote and told him to wait. I went to the small office that Deacon was in and went to see what he had. Deacon had given his man a pad and had him write the information down. I nodded as Deacon stood and we went to the side of the room.

"Okay, let's see what we got," I said and we compared the two pads. The information was different. "As I figured. One of them knows and the other is looking for cash."

I went to the man, "What's your name?"

"Kenny."

"Okay, Kenny, how do you know this information?"

"Sal and I were friends. He told me he was going to be hiding and where, just in case his girlfriend came looking for him."

"Rasman had a girlfriend?"

"Yeah, he called her Brigitte, she was German. He said she lived in Vegas and they would see each other once a week."

"A man who lived in the tunnels, goes to see a woman once a week? What did she do for a living?"

73

"She worked street corners, if you know what I mean."

"A hooker and a homeless man? That's a pair. Have you ever met this woman?"

"No, just what Sal told me."

I looked at Deacon and smiled. "How's that sound to you?"

"Like a fun dream." Deacon turned to Kenny. "Her name was Brigitte? Last name?"

"Don't know."

"Never saw her and don't know her last name? How do you know that she exists, beyond what Sal supposedly told you? Maybe he lied," I said.

"I just have to believe Sal, that's all. Why would he lie to me, we were friends?"

I could have mentioned the man was a scoundrel and a criminal. I decided that Kenny wasn't giving us much. "Okay, if we find Rasman at this address, I'll see you receive the money. But, if you're lying to us, I'm sure my friend here, Detective DeAngelo, will be wanting to question you further."

Kenny didn't change his expression. He still looked clueless. I went out of the room and to the other man waiting patiently where I left him. Deacon followed after telling Kenny to go back to his room.

"Okay, what's your name?" I asked the man still sitting at the desk.

He jumped and said, "Eric Finn."

"Eric tell me how you know this is where Rasman is at?"

"He told me."

"That doesn't tell me much. Why did he tell you this is his location?"

"He trusted me to know where he was, in case something happened to him."

"How does knowing where he is help him?"

"He said if he didn't contact me in two more days, I was to tell the police where he was at."

I said to Deacon, "Now that I can believe. Rasman would hide out unless he was found. With Eric waiting for word and receiving none, we could find his body. Makes sense."

"Do I get the money?" Eric asked.

"Not until we verify that Sal is at this location. If he is, I'll see you get the money."

"Oh, can I get an advance?" he said sheepishly.

I was trying to hold in a laugh and took a twenty out of my pocket and handed it to him. "Don't buy any drugs with this or you'll lose the rest. Understand?"

"I don't do drugs, but I do have a beer every now and then."

At least he was being honest. I have a beer every now and then, too. "Okay, don't drink too much. Save a little. I'll let you know what we find. Go back to your room now, and thanks."

He stood and left the room. "I have to believe this story over the girlfriend. Shall we check here first?" I said.

"I'll call Warren and have him meet us there with back up." He pulled his cell phone and placed the call.

Buck came back to us and I filled him in on the incident. "So, are we going to get him?" he asked.

"As soon as Deacon gets organized. Which could take a while," I replied.

He heard me. "You know I don't need to take you. This is police business, smart ass," he said and started to leave the office. Buck and I followed.

I had the paper with the address, so Deacon had to come back to me to get it. "I may not give it to you for that last comment," I said with a smile.

"And I stand by my statement. Now, the address please."

"Since you said please." I handed him the paper and he went off.

Buck looked at me, "You did remember the address?"

"Of course, he called me a smart ass, not a dumb ass."

"Sometimes I wonder. Shall we go?" he asked and we went to my car. I followed Deacon out onto the road, and over to a house near McLeod Drive and E. Russell Road.

"How can Rasman afford a place in this area?" Buck asked.

Wiseguy Murders

"Most likely a friend's house. Whatever, the address is real, so Eric may have been correct."

Deacon pulled up at the curb, just down from the house, and waited for back-up. Warren and two patrol cars pulled up and Deacon got the warrant he told Warren to file before coming out. With the paper, Deacon led the charge. They got to the house and banged on the door. After a moment, a woman answered the door. She looked shocked at all the cops on her porch.

"Ma'am, we have a search warrant to locate one Sal Rasman. Do you know him?" he asked as his officers streamed into the building.

She still looked shocked and now perplexed. "Sal isn't here right now. Why do you want him?"

"It's for his protection. We know there are men after him and we want to keep him alive. Where did he go?"

She paused and looked like she was thinking. Deacon was waiting, which I know he hated to do. He wasn't a patient person when it came to crime.

"He went out for food. We were getting low and he said he had to get out of the house. That was an hour ago. He should have been back by now."

I could tell that worried Deacon.

Chapter 12

Deacon called for all his men to go back to their cars and drive to the next block and wait for his call. They all streamed out as fast as they came in. Deacon asked the woman to go into the next room and relax. He turned to me and said, "We can wait for another half hour then I'll have to put out a BOLO for him."

He went to the other room that must have been the living room and sat in front of the woman on a foot stool. "What's your name?" he asked.

"Brigitte," she replied and Deacon looked to me and grinned.

"Do you just live here or do you own this house?"

"No, it belongs to a relative of mine, Carmine. He's out of town and lets me stay here."

"Does he know that Sal is staying here?"

"I told him he was."

Wiseguy Murders

"What does Carmine do for work?"

"Something to do with running, he said once when he didn't think I was listening."

"What kind of running does he do?" Deacon asked.

"I think it has something to do with math, because he said his business runs numbers."

Deacon stood turning to Warren, Buck and me. "Crap, her friend works for the mob, but whose? If he's in with the people who want Rasman, then we can start looking for shallow graves in the desert. Romanny doesn't do illegal business anymore, so we have a narrow choice of families left."

Brigitte was sitting listening, then she said, "Are you talking about my uncle, Rico Romanny?"

We all turned slowly, stunned at what she said. Deacon went back to her and sat. "Your uncle is Rico Romanny?"

"Yes, he's my father's brother," she replied.

"Who's your father?"

"Marco Petrochelli, they're half-brothers actually. He lives in Arizona, due to his health. I see him once in a while when I go out to visit. He hasn't seen Uncle Rico in years, and he doesn't know where he's at. I don't either. I haven't seen Uncle Rico in years. I'm not sure if he's even still alive."

Deacon didn't give her any updates on Uncle Rico. "Has your father been looking for your Uncle lately?"

"Not that I know of. My father and Uncle Rico aren't friendly with each other. I do remember Daddy saying that Uncle Rico stole money from him. But, I never heard if they worked that out."

Deacon looked to me and said quietly, "That's a good reason to find Uncle Rico." He turned back to the woman, "Do you know if your father could be here in Vegas?"

"He wouldn't come here without telling me. I'm sure of that."

I moved forward and asked, "Brigitte, would you like to go see your Uncle Rico?"

Her eyes grew wider and she said, "You know where he's at?"

"I have an idea, and I was planning on visiting him with a friend. If you'd like to come along, I'll see if it can be arranged."

81

"I'd love that, yes."

Deacon spoke up, "Jim, if her father is the one looking for Romanny, would it be wise to take her to him?"

I smiled at the woman and said, "Brigitte, I'd be happy to take you with us to see your uncle, but it's important that you tell no one where he is. There are men looking to possibly harm your uncle and if they knew where he was, they might kill him." I was spreading it on a little thick, but I wanted to impress on her the importance of keeping his location secret.

"Oh, my goodness. I wouldn't want him to be harmed. I'll tell no one."

"Not even your father, if you talk to him. That's important, too."

"I can't tell Dad?"

"Not right now, but I'll tell you when it's safe," I said.

"Okay, my lips are sealed." She did that motion with her finger of locking her lips. It was cute coming from her. She was in her late twenties and fairly attractive in a child-like way.

Deacon spoke now, "You said Sal went to get groceries? Where do you usually shop?"

"Albertsons. It's where I always go. I told Sal that he could go somewhere else, Albertsons is always so busy with people and he didn't like being around people. You know he's homeless, don't you?"

"Yes, we do. And we're trying to help him. But, right now there are bad men after him and we need to find him first, before they do." Deacon turned to Warren and said, "Go send up Rasman's photo from the shelter on the LEIN and put out a BOLO for him. Send a couple uniforms to Albertsons and see if they spot him."

Greg Warren left the room as Deacon said, "Brigitte, what did Sal say when he asked to stay with you?"

"Well, he said he needed to lay low for a while. He didn't tell me from who, but he was scared at the time. I was worried for him, so I asked my step-brother, Carmine, if he could stay here. Carmine asked who he was and I told him. He seemed interested in Sal and we talked about him for a while. Carmine said it was good, so I told Sal he could stay."

"Did Sal ever mention a man by the name of Martin Scarpo?"

"Scarpo? Yeah, I heard the name mentioned once when Sal was talking to someone on the phone.

Wiseguy Murders

Sal seemed concerned about this man called Scarpo. He was saying that they found Scarpo instead of him. I didn't hear much more, sorry."

Deacon sat for a moment, saying nothing. He looked to me and finally spoke, "I think I have everything up to now figured out. But, who wants Rasman and for what reason? Guess we wait to hear from Rasman."

I turned and went to the window at the front of the house and looked out. The street was vacant except for my car parked down from the house. Warren must have left with Deacon's unmarked car. Why they call them unmarked, I never could figure. They stuck out like a cop car even with no lights showing. If Sal came back right now, he wouldn't know there were police in the house. Well, one cop, Deacon. Everyone else was hiding on the next block waiting for Deacon to call.

I was leaning on the window ledge watching the street when a Chevy Suburban pulled up. Four men with guns exited the vehicle. I yelled to Deacon to call his men. He came to the window as the men were spreading out around the house. He pulled his cell phone and called the squad leader and said to get the hell back now. We had men with guns.

We ran back into the living room and I held out my hand to Brigitte and pulled her up.

"Do you have a basement?" I asked.

She pointed to a door. I took her there and opened the door, there were stairs going down and I gently guided her to them. "Go down there and hide until I come and get you." She ran down the stairs as I pulled my Glock and turned to Deacon. Buck had his weapon out already for the fight, as did Deacon.

"Once more into the breach, dear friends," I said.

*

Chapter 13

Buck and I headed to the back door as Deacon stationed himself by the front door. His back-up men would be roaring up shortly, so we just needed to hold off the attackers till then. I could hear a noise at the kitchen door, the knob turning slowly, finding it was locked. I knew the back-up men would be concentrating on the front as they arrived, so Buck and I had to stop the bad guys coming in from the back.

Suddenly, the glass window of the door was smashed in and an arm came in through the broken pane to unlock it. I fired a shot at the door—not aiming at the men—just to startle them. They returned fire through the door. Buck and I were already on the floor next to the snack bar. I felt safe there. I could hear shots coming from the front of the house. Either Deacon's men had arrived or he was firing on the criminals.

Fortunately, our intruders figured whoever shot at them were hit by their shots and they busted the door open. The two thugs came rushing in and stopped when they saw the room was empty. I peeked around the bottom of the snack bar as Buck came up over the top. He yelled to freeze, but they didn't. I shot from below and took down one of them. Buck was blasting at the other, knocking him off his feet.

I heard a couple more gunshots from the front and then it went quiet. Deacon's back-up came in through the back door and stopped, giving us a chance to identify ourselves. There was more yelling going on up front as Buck and I went back to see how Deacon made out.

He was standing looking at the two men sitting on the floor, one with his hands on his head, the other holding a wound on his side. The back-up men who were checking the vehicle came in and started to cuff the perps. A couple of them went to the kitchen to help the other men. Buck and I didn't check to see if the perps were alive or not before we left the kitchen.

"Well, that was fun," Deacon said. I went to the door to the basement and called down to Brigitte.

"It's okay to come up now," I said loudly.

I heard her say, "Who are you?"

I smiled and answered, "I'm with the police, and you're safe now."

"How do I know you are who you say you are?" she asked.

I grinned at Buck standing next to me, listening. "Guess I have to go get her." I went down the steps and found her standing in the middle of the basement looking frightened. She saw who I was and came running over to me. I took her up the stairs and had her sit on the couch.

Deacon came over and asked her, "Do you know where Carmine is at?"

"I have an address where he is staying in Bullhead City."

"Get it for me, please," he said and turned to me. "Carmine knew that Rasman was staying here. No one else that we know of knew. So, he's a big link to this and why these men came here."

Brigitte brought a slip of paper and gave it to Deacon. He looked at it and turned to Warren who came in after the back-up. "Greg, have Bullhead PD go to this address." Deacon asked Brigitte for Carmine's full name. She said his name was Carmine Petrochelli. That surprised Deacon. "So Carmine is related to you?"

"He's sort of my step-brother. My father's second wife's son."

"Big family," Deacon mugged. Then he turned to Warren. "Have them pick up Carmine Petrochelli, so we can bring him back here. He's now a suspect for murder."

Warren went off and Deacon turned back to Brigitte. "What all did you tell your step-brother about Sal?"

"I told him Sal was homeless and needed a place to hide out for a few days. He asked me why he had to hide out and I told him that Sal was afraid of some people looking for him. Sal used to work for my uncle's family years ago and felt they wanted to find my uncle."

"You're talking about Uncle Rico."

"Yeah. Carmine seemed interested and said that Sal could stay as long as he wanted."

"Did Sal know Carmine owns this house?"

"No, I never mentioned Carmine to Sal." She replied.

Deacon turned to us. "So, Carmine, her step-brother from her father's wife, letting Sal, who worked for her uncle Rico, stay as long as he wanted? Sounds like a family plot to me," Deacon said. "Okay, Carmine tells his step-father that Sal is hiding out in this house, which is a wild coincidence.

Wiseguy Murders

Petrochelli, the mob father, sends his men to grab Sal to find his half-brother Rico. Are you two confused yet?"

"It's hurting my head. This is becoming one good Monty Python movie." I laughed.

"And Sal is still missing. But I think we have enough info as to why someone wants Sal. Now, I don't know if we can go question Petrochelli, the mob father. He's in Arizona and we have no proof that he's involved."

"Angelo and I can still go talk to Romanny, maybe he'll be interested in knowing someone may be after him."

"Well, I hope it doesn't start a mob war. Maybe one of the perps we caught today will talk. Let's go back to interrogate them."

Deacon asked Warren to assign a couple officers to watch the house in case Sal came back and to keep an eye on Brigitte. Buck and I went to my car as Deacon went to his.

We met up at the precinct and went in to find the uninjured perp sitting in interrogation room two. His partner was taken under guard to the hospital to remove a bullet. Our perp, David Cross, was sitting quietly as Deacon entered the room. Buck and I went into observation, since Deacon wanted to talk alone.

"David Cross. You have been arrested for attacking a private home with a weapon and firing at police officers. Not looking good for you. Two of your men are dead, and your buddy is having a bullet removed from his shoulder. You were lucky that you gave up before I shot you, too. Or my men shot you. That was smart. Now, why don't you be smart and tell me who you were after at the house."

Cross sat quietly, not saying a word. "That's all right, we know you were after Sal Rasman," Deacon said. "We also know you work for Marco Petrochelli. He's not going to be happy that you failed in your mission."

Cross raised his eyebrows a bit when Deacon mentioned Petrochelli. I figured Deacon was taking a chance and putting things together for the man.

"Come on, Cross, talk to me and maybe we'll let you get away without Petrochelli knowing you screwed up. You could start elsewhere. But only if you talk to us first."

Cross sat quietly for a moment. Then he said, "What makes you think whoever hired me won't kill me, even if you hide me?"

"Hired you? Are you saying you don't work for Marco Petrochelli?" Deacon asked.

Wiseguy Murders

"I don't even know who this Marco Petrochelli is you're talking about. I work for whoever pays the most and that wasn't the person you call Marco Petrochelli."

Deacon turned away from Cross and faced the mirror. I could see he had a look of annoyance on his face.

*

Chapter 14

Deacon turned back to Cross, "Fine, then tell me who hired you to find Rasman."

He sat quietly thinking, then said, "I'd like my lawyer now."

I was waiting for Deacon to punch the guy out. He didn't.

"Okay, you can get your lawyer. But you know you'll go down for attacking officers of the law with a weapon. And, unlawful entrance of a private home with intent to kidnap."

"You can't prove I was there to kidnap anyone."

"Then why were you there? Certainly not to sell magazine subscriptions. The only person in that house you would have wanted was Sal Rasman. Unless you were there to kidnap Brigitte Petrochelli?"

"Geez, how many Petrochellis are there?"

Wiseguy Murders

"I've only mentioned two, do you know of more? Maybe Carmine Petrochelli?" The man had a look of discomfort on his face. "Did Carmine Petrochelli hire you to nab Rasman?"

"As I said, I want my lawyer," Cross said, then sat back and folded his arms over his chest.

Deacon went to the door, then said, "Okay, last chance. Talk to me or be charged."

Cross said nothing. Deacon started out the door, told the cop guarding it to take Cross back to holding and then came over to us. He entered observation and plopped down on a chair. "Damn, I'd like to find the person who started this 'I want my lawyer' law."

"So, he's lawyered up, you just have to wait now," I said. "Or, you could go chat to the guy in the hospital. Maybe you could get him to talk."

Deacon was quiet for a moment. I let him think, I knew it was a slow process for him. He stood and said, "Let's get out of here and go watch some nurses." He left the room, Buck and I followed him. Buck was grinning, probably at the thought of going to watch nurses.

Deacon told one of his detectives where he was going and we went out to our cars and over to the hospital. I wasn't fond of hospitals, they bred disease, even though they are supposed to cure them. More people get sick visiting hospitals than anywhere else.

We arrived at the room of the less fortunate bad guy. The cop sitting at the door stood when he saw Deacon coming towards him.

"Lieutenant, everything is quiet. No problems with him. I think he's still sleeping, at least he was the last time I checked on him."

"Thanks, Hosler. Just stay vigilant," Deacon said and went into the room followed by me. Buck said he was going to help guard the door. I knew better. The room was across from the nurse's station and there were a number of them gathered there. They were checking out Buck as much as he was checking out them.

Deacon went to the bed where the man was resting. He had his eyes open and watched us approach. He didn't look happy. I guess the drugs he was on weren't working.

"Harvey Verstadt, I'm Detective DeAngelo. I hope you're feeling better. Sorry I had to shoot you, but you did fire at me. Which didn't make me happy, and it's cause for you to be prosecuted for attempted murder of a police officer. Not a good charge to have hanging over you. Oh, and there's the matter of breaking and entering with intent to kidnap. I'm sure we can find a few other charges to throw at you."

The man was looking even less happy now. "What do you want, cop?" he said softly and with a pained expression.

"I'd like very much to know who sent you to nab Sal Rasman? That's all. Maybe I can even see my way to get your charges lowered to just B&E. I'll forgive you firing at me."

"You want me to tell you who hired us? Are you crazy? I wouldn't talk if I knew. Besides, Dave Cross handled all the hiring for us. So, I don't know who hired us."

"Well, you must have heard who you were after."

"Yeah, it was that Rasman guy you mentioned. We were supposed to grab him and take him somewhere. Again, you'll have to get that from Cross."

"Do you know anyone with the last name of Petrochelli?"

He went silent, and looked away. "No," was all he said.

"Well, we think it was someone named Petrochelli who hired you. He's not someone to mess with and he may not be happy to know that you ratted him out."

Verstadt just about came out of the bed. "Hey, I didn't rat out anyone, least of all Petrochelli. I'm a dead man if you spread that I mentioned him."

"Well, I could say you were uncooperative if you'd just give us a few more details. That might spare your life."

Verstadt settled back onto his pillow and scowled. "Not giving me much choice, are you? I want to see a lawyer."

I could almost see the veins popping out of Deacon's neck as he held his temper. "You want a lawyer, fine. But, I'll see that you are pegged as a rat. See if your lawyer can get you out of that."

"Damn you, cop. You can't lie about something like that."

"You admitted to knowing Petrochelli. You fingered him. That's all I have to say about this attempt to grab Rasman."

"Okay, what do you want?" he whined.

"What were you told to do?"

Wiseguy Murders

He paused for a short while, Deacon waited. "We were told to go to that house and take Sal Rasman out and then go to some house down in Bullhead City. That's all I know, honestly."

Deacon looked back to me and said, "Bullhead City. That's where Carmine is staying. So he must have been in on it."

He turned back to Verstadt, "You don't know who you were supposed to deliver him to?"

"You don't listen very well, I said Cross knew that, not me. Get him to tell you. Now, are you going to leave me out of this?"

Deacon smiled and said, "No." Then he turned and headed to the door.

"Hey, you lied!" Verstadt yelled.

Deacon turned his head back and said, "Yes, I did." He and I left the room.

Buck was over at the nurse's station talking up a couple young candy stripers. I figured they were half his age, so they were safe. Doesn't hurt to talk to attractive females as long as you don't get involved.

"Buck, are you going to stay here?" I called as I went past him. He grinned and said something to the girls, they giggled and he followed me.

"So what did you find out?" he asked, catching up to me.

I told him what went on in the room with Verstadt as he listened. We went to our cars and drove back to the precinct.

Deacon was stopped by another detective in the squad room, who said, "Cross is out on bail."

Deacon just stood, not saying a word. Then he said quietly, "Why?"

"His lawyer rushed it through, friend of some judge, I guess. He left about ten minutes ago."

I could see Deacon's veins growing again. He went to his office as Buck and I followed.

"Close the door," he stated harshly. I did, and he let loose a long string of expletives that I never heard from him before.

*

Chapter 15

I looked at Buck and said, "Gee, dear, our little boy is becoming an adult."

Deacon gave me the finger and sat at this desk.

"Did that feel good?" I asked.

He smiled and said, "Yes, it did. Something I can't do at home with the baby around."

"I think PJ is still a little too young to learn those words," I responded.

"Yeah, well Lynn doesn't like to hear those words either. So I come down here, close my door and let loose."

"Is everything all right? Are you feeling the pressure?"

"As I told you a while back, I'm a little frustrated. What with the added responsibilities of this job and the baby up all hours of the night. Yeah, I'm feeling pressure. Now my suspect has walked out with the blessing of the courts. It's a losing battle. When are you going to talk with Romanny?"

I saw how Deacon switched the conversation from him. "I'm going to talk with Angelo in the morning, see if he can get us in."

"What about Brigitte, you going to take her?" he asked.

"Most likely, she may be an asset to have along."

"Let me know how it comes out. I'm curious to know if Romanny has any idea that someone may be looking for him."

"I'm not sure what we'll find out. If this Romanny has been in hiding all these years, maybe he's been out of touch with everything mob related," I said.

"I doubt that. I'm sure Romanny has been watching the waters for a ripple to take back over. I doubt he knows about Rasman, since Rasman has been homeless for so long."

"I'll watch to see what reaction we get when we mention Rasman. Maybe Romanny will send some of his boys out to find him too."

Wiseguy Murders

"As I said, I don't want a mob war starting. Try to be diplomatic if you can."

"I'm all about diplomatic, now Angelo, he may not be so diplomatic. Although he may be respectful since his mother is married to the boss of a mob family."

"Just tread lightly. Only try to get information on who may have murdered Scarpo and who may be after Rasman." Deacon sighed and sat back.

"Tired?" I asked him.

"A little worn. I love my daughter, but I can do without the all-night crying."

"Try earplugs," I said with a grin.

"Doesn't work, Lynn pushes me out of bed to take care of the baby."

"Well, it's something that will last for a short time, until the baby grows out of it. I'm going to my office to see what my baby is doing. At least she doesn't cry in the night," I said, then, "no snide comments from you."

Deacon grinned and told us to leave him to his own problems. I took Buck out to the car and drove to the shelter where he had left his car.

Bob Moats

I dropped him off and said, "I'll talk to you later, I have to get with Angelo to organize our attack on the mob." He waved and went off to his car.

I drove to my building and parked in the back. I didn't see Fred or his dog. Fred's car was gone, so I figured he may be at the shelter helping out. I thought that Willy must be with Penny since he wasn't in the dog pen. I went in the back door, setting off Lacey's cow bell. It made me laugh every time I heard it. I waved to the security camera at the back door and headed up front. I entered the lobby and Tracey was at Lacey's desk.

"Where's Lacey?" I asked the young girl, spotting Willy lying on the desk, sleeping. He put his head up when he heard me.

"She and your wife went to do some shopping. They said they'd be back before we close."

"Fine, I'll be in my office." I left the lobby and went to my office by way of Lynn's office. She was at her desk. "Do you have anything on the Frisard's case?" I asked about the little man who hired us to find out who was fooling around with his wife. I sat in her client chair.

"I followed the wife around and she met with about three men. I got pictures of all of them, and I'm waiting for Frisard to come in."

Wiseguy Murders

"Was Hartwell one of the men?" I asked about the man who came to us about Frisard possibly murdering him for messing with Frisard's wife.

"Luckily, he wasn't. I don't know who the other men were, but you said that the wife knew Frisard came to us to follow her. So why did she still go to meet these men?"

I thought on that for a moment. "Yeah, she should know better than to be seen with other men. Maybe she knows her husband may do something bad, like murder them. It could be her way of getting rid of her husband."

"That's a thought. I'll see what Frisard says when he gets a look at the photos. If he knows the men, I'll find out what his intentions are. Divorce, maybe?"

"Whatever, let me know the outcome. I have to go relax and get my head into my case. It's getting complicated, with lots of players." I stood and left her office and went around to mine. Willy followed me to my desk after he spotted me in the hallway. I picked him up, put him on the desk, then he plopped down, huffed, and closed his eyes. I felt like doing that, too. I sat back in my chair and closed my eyes.

I was suddenly being shaken, and opened my eyes to find Penny standing over me. "Just like you to be sleeping while the world is falling apart," she said with a grin.

I looked at my watch and realized I had slept for about an hour. Willy was standing on my desk looking at me. "Dumb dog, you could have warned me she was here." I looked at my wife, "So, you kidnapped Lacey to go shopping? Did you make her carry your packages?"

"No, since I took Tracey to get new clothes, I figured Lacey may need a new wardrobe, too."

"Well, that's noble of you to think of others. When are you taking me for a new wardrobe?"

"You can suffer with the clothes you have. I'm done with shopping for a while."

"What? You're not going shopping anymore?" I said, surprised.

"Oh, no, I'll still shop, but I'm giving it a rest for now. I wore myself out enough shopping for the girls to last me a couple months."

"This is a momentous occasion. It's getting late, shall we close up the office and go home and celebrate?"

"Don't get any ideas, buster. I'm not celebrating the way you want to." She turned and went out. I put Willy on the floor and he ran out after her.

I went out into the hallway, it was quiet. I checked the other offices and no one was in. I went out to the lobby and told Lacey to get Tracey and go home.

She smiled and said, "I'm going home to try on my new clothes." She looked to Penny and said, "Thank you so much for them."

Penny smiled as Lacey gathered the packages on the counter and went out the front to the outer lobby where Tracey was and I saw them both leave the building.

I turned to Penny, "Yep, you are such a nice person. Got any gifts for me?"

"I am a gift, so appreciate me." She smiled and went out the front door, leaving me to lock up.

*

Bob Moats

Chapter 16

We did our usual nightly routine; beer, chips and TV. We finally crawled into bed and cuddled.

I couldn't sleep thinking about going to meet an exiled ex-mob boss who it seemed everyone was after. I also thought that this may not have anything to do with Romanny and it was something totally different. I always did this when I wanted to sleep. I thought too much. It was hard to stop the brain from putting on little plays in my head. Penny was already asleep and I pulled my arm out from under her, slowly so not to wake her. She mumbled to quit moving, so I did.

I thought about the phone call I made to Angelo earlier explaining about Romanny's niece. Angelo was more than happy to take her along. He said he'd call in the morning to arrange to meet with Romanny.

I guess I fell asleep a short time later, because Penny was bouncing out of the bed to her bathroom, waking me up. I sat up and looked at Willy sitting up on the bed watching me.

Wiseguy Murders

"Stop looking so cute, you mongrel," I said and swung out of bed. I went to my bathroom and did my morning duties. It was good that Penny and I each had our own bathrooms. The smell in mine would not please her. I sprayed with a scented aerosol and went out to get dressed. Penny was already in the kitchen getting breakfast. I decided to skip my morning toast, I didn't want to go see a mob boss and have to use the bathroom.

Penny went off with a kiss and took Willy. I gathered my equipment and went to my car. I drove over to Angelo's restaurant and parked myself because it was too early for valet. I went in the employee entrance since the restaurant wasn't open yet, and found Angelo sitting at a table in the dining room having breakfast.

"Mr. R., you want some eggs and sausage?" Angelo asked.

"No thanks, my friend. I don't want food in my stomach before we go see Romanny. Have you had a chance to get an audience with the man?" I said and sat at the table.

"Sure did. He was more than happy to see me. He actually remembers my mom," Angelo beamed.

"Did you mention about possibly bringing his niece?"

"That thrilled him even more so. He hasn't seen the girl in over fifteen years, so this should be a nice visit. He said we should go to the new mob museum and wait for his car to pick us up," Angelo said, between bites of his food.

"Well, we're going in style. I presume we'll be searched, too."

"Good idea not to take your gun with you." He laughed.

I would feel naked without my Glock, but better to be safe than in cement boots. "No problem, I'll leave it in my car. Are we going to pick up Brigitte before we go to the museum?"

"We can do that. I'll have my driver swing by to get her. We have an hour before we are to meet the car, so shall we pick up the niece?"

"I'll call Deacon so he can warn his officers watching her. I don't want to get shot by the good guys either."

"Make your call while I finish my breakfast."

I pulled my cell phone and hit speed dial. Deacon came on and I explained what we were going to do. He said he'd call off the heat on Brigitte and we could take her. We finished our call after Deacon wished us good luck.

Wiseguy Murders

I put my phone back in my pocket and leaned on the table. "Deacon said we could go pick up Brigitte. Have you ever met Romanny before?"

Angelo wiped his mouth with a napkin and dropped it on his plate. "Nope, never met him—that I know of. I was very young when my family, run by my father, were on halfway friendly terms with Romanny's family. They stayed away from each other and never caused problems. Rico Romanny was a fair boss from what my mother used to say. He kept his word on deals and never shot a man who didn't need shooting," he said with a big laugh. "Romanny is now what they call a Mustache Pete, an old-fashioned or older generation Mafiosi. He probably still goes by the old rules. Not like these corporation gangs they have now. I'm sure Romanny will be decent to us. He'll really enjoy seeing his niece."

"Yep, she's a looker. But, I'm not saying Romanny would have any thoughts about his own niece," I said.

"Romanny has to be in his nineties by now. I doubt he'd be chasing young women." Angelo stood and continued, "Shall we go pick up this young woman?"

We both went out the back door and found Angelo's car. It was similar to my mini-limo that was given to me by Angelo's step-father, Gino. I was surprised to see Mario, our informant in the Santa Murder case. He brought down the hitman ring and the leader. I remember him saying Angelo was going to find work for him, I guess being a driver was part of that job.

"Mario, good to see you again. How are you holding up?" I said as he held open the door to the back of the limo.

"Doing good, Mr. Richards. Angelo has me working hard for him," he said with a big grin.

"Glad to hear it." I got in the car next to Angelo and Mario closed the door.

I didn't want to ask what kind of work Angelo had Mario doing. If Angelo was forming his own little family, I think I didn't want to know. Angelo didn't say, so I didn't ask.

I gave Mario the directions for the house where Brigitte was staying and he drove off. I sat back as Angelo said, "When we get there, let me do the talking. I will ask you questions about what your case involves, but don't talk any more than you need to. Keep it brief. Romanny can be impatient with people from what I know, so we'll just feel this out."

"It was your cousin who was murdered, so I'm sure you'll know what you want to find out. I'm just here as a friend of yours, so take the lead."

Wiseguy Murders

We arrived at the house and found Brigitte standing on the porch. She came bouncing over as Mario got out, opening the door for her. She got in and sat across from us.

"Angelo, this is Brigitte Petrochelli. Brigitte, this is my friend, Angelo DeMarko," I said.

"Petrochelli? You related to Marco Petrochelli?" Angelo asked.

"Yes, he's my father," she replied. "Rico Romanny is my father's half-brother. So, I guess that still makes him my uncle."

"Well, when I talked to him, he certainly remembered you. Looks like we have three families getting together for a nice visit." Angelo looked at me and smiled. "The Petrochelli's weren't real friendly with the Romanny family. I remember my second father talking about the problems they had. But that was well in the past, hopefully all is good now."

"I'm hoping this meeting will be friendly," I said, as we approached the mob museum to be picked up.

*

Chapter 17

We pulled into the parking lot of what once was the Las Vegas Post Office and Court House. The building had been sold by the federal government to the city for a dollar, under the stipulation that it be renovated to its original state. A group of people worked hard to create the Mob Museum, also called the National Museum of Organized Crime and Law Enforcement. They even purchased the original bloodstained wall from the St. Valentine's Day massacre in Chicago. I hadn't been to the museum yet, I'd have to take Penny to see it.

We pulled around until we saw a limo even bigger than Angelo's. We pulled up next to it as two very big men got out and came to us. Mario came around and opened the door for us to get out. We let Brigitte go first, then Angelo exited, then I scooted out. I wasn't quite as important as the others.

The big bruisers started to frisk me and Angelo. One of them went to Brigitte. "You touch her and you will deal with me," Angelo growled. Brigitte had on a tight, short dress that would show if she had a weapon. The man walked around, eyeing her, then moved back. The other man said to get in the car. We did after Angelo told Mario to take the car back until he called.

I was surprised to see all the windows were blacked out. I guessed it was so we didn't know where we were going. We drove around for what seemed an hour, I presumed to shake any tail or to possibly confuse us so we wouldn't know which direction we were heading.It didn't really matter, Angelo had already given me the address.

We finally slowed and turned into what seemed like a driveway. I could hear gates opening and then we drove on. The car stopped and our door opened. We were asked to exit the car. My eyes adjusted back to the sunshine and I could see a humongous mansion in front of us. There were four men at the entrance with automatic weapons I hoped weren't going to be used on us.

The front door flew open and a young woman, possibly in her thirties, came out to us. "Welcome, friends. I presume you are Angelo," she said to him.

"I am, and you are?" he asked back.

"Celeste Romanny, granddaughter of Rico Romanny. I was asked to bring you to my grandfather."

Bob Moats

I was surprised she didn't say Godfather. She turned and we followed her into the gigantic building. She led us through a vestibule and into a hallway that seemed to go on forever. She went to a door off the side and opened it. She stood back and motioned us to enter.

It was a huge library, which reminded me of the one we were in out in New York, when we visited Gino Traviano, Angelo's step-father. Then we saw him, Rico Romanny. At least I think it was him. He was very old and reminded me of Marlon Brando in *The Godfather,* only greyer in the hair and with a thin pencil moustache. He was very wrinkled and his eyes were bloodshot. Mostly from age I assumed. He sat in a high-back chair in the middle of the room, with a blanket covering his legs. There were two very large men standing about five feet behind him—his lieutenants, I figured. On our right, at a very large desk sat a man, also silver-haired, with a bright white smile. He was dressed in what looked to be Armani, and had his shirt open to reveal a silver chain and a crucifix. He had rings on most of his fingers that glittered as he moved his hands while playing with a crystal globe. I was wondering why he was smiling.

"Come to me my friends, you are most welcome," Rico said with a husky voice that surprised me. We moved forward, I stayed behind Angelo as Brigitte walked next to him. We stopped about five feet from him and waited.

115

Wiseguy Murders

He held his hand out towards Brigitte and said, "Child, come to me."

She moved to him and took his hand. "You are as beautiful as I remember you years ago. I last saw you when I moved my family from New York to Vegas. My health needed the dry air. Sit Bambina, here, next to me." There were three chairs near his and she sat on the one at his right.

"I'm so happy to see you. I don't get to see much of my real family, other than my son and granddaughter. I'm glad you came."

"I'm happy to see you also, Uncle," she replied.

He got a big smile and asked, "How have you been all these years, and what are you doing with your life? Nothing illegal I hope?"

"Oh no, I work as a model and demonstrator at the big convention center on the strip. I show cars and products for companies that have trade shows there."

They chatted for a couple minutes about her and I noticed he never asked about her father, Marco. Angelo and I just waited.

Finally, he looked to us, mostly Angelo, and said, "Angelo, come closer."

Angelo moved to the man and stopped in front of him. Angelo spoke, "So good to finally meet you, don Romanny. My mother has talked about you in the past. All good, of course."

"Ah, your mother, the sainted Frances. How is she doing?" He took on a glow and straightened in his chair.

"She's doing very good for a woman in her eighties. Exercises and works in her garden. Keeps fit."

"I heard she married again, the third time now?"

Angelo seemed cautious, I didn't know if Romanny and the Travianos were on friendly terms.

"Yes, she married Gino Traviano. They are in New York, now."

Romanny sat back and smiled. "Gino. Yes, we ran as teens in New York. He was a Compare to me. Good friend and hell-raiser, as I remember. How is he doing? He's not into drug dealing, I hope."

"Oh, no. He detests drugs and prostitution. Numbers and gambling are his earners."

"Good. He was an honorable man," he said with a wistful smile, most likely thinking of days past. Then he looked back to Angelo, "I last I saw you when you were no higher than my waist. How are you doing? You live here in Vegas?"

"Yes, sir. I left the life and came out here to start out on my own." He motioned to me and continued, "My good friend here, Jim Richards, gave me a job as a bodyguard in his firm, then he helped me financially, to open my own restaurant, Mama Mia. It's doing very well."

Romanny looked at me, I felt a chill. Not that he was giving me the evil eye or anything, but it was like having someone very important acknowledge you.

"Jim, come closer." I moved to him and stopped next to Angelo.

"You are a friend to Angelo. That is good. Angelo said you had a firm, what kind?"

I didn't know if Angelo told him I was a private investigator, I glanced at Angelo and said, "I have an investigating firm, mostly following cheating spouses and investigating the occasional murder." I tensed up waiting to see what reaction I'd get.

"Ah, a P.I., like Magnum. I loved that show when it was on."

I let out the breath I was holding and relaxed.

*

Chapter 18

"So, Angelo was a bodyguard for you. Now he's a big restaurateur. Good. I don't get out much, but I will have to come eat one time."

Angelo smiled and said, "If you don't feel like going out, we deliver and cater now."

Romanny laughed and said, "I'll keep that in mind. Now, sit, we aren't formal here."

Angelo and I pulled up the other two chairs and sat. I glanced over to the man at the desk. He was still smiling. I hoped he wasn't sizing us up for caskets.

"So, Angelo, when you called, it was a pleasure. You said you had to talk to me about an important matter. Speak to me."

Wiseguy Murders

Angelo cleared his throat and said, "Well, don Romanny, my friend Jim became involved in a murder at a homeless shelter he helped build for the unfortunates of Vegas. It was an old motel that he and his wife, along with a preacher, bought and converted."

"Nice you share with your wife, Jim," he said.

"You may or may not know her, Penny Wickens," I said.

His eyes lit up and he turned to the man at the desk. "You hear this, Antonio, Jim is married to Penny Wickens."

The man grinned now and said in a gravelly voice, "I read about that, Papa. I recognized Mr. Richards when he came in the room."

I now knew why he was smiling at me. That made me feel better.

"Mi piace, che è così buono." Romany said. I'd have to ask Angelo what he said later. "This is a special day. You should have brought her with you, Jim."

"She's working on her show right now, but I can bring her when she's off." I hoped Penny wouldn't mind coming for a visit.

"You do that, or I'll send my men to find you," he growled, then laughed. "I'm sorry, Angelo, continue with what you were saying."

"Well, Jim told me who was murdered at the shelter, it was a cousin of mine, Martin Scarpo."

"Not good, was this a burn?"

"I don't think it was a hit aimed at him. We think the killer, or killers, found my cousin by mistake, they were after Sal Rasman. You should know him."

"Ah, that gavone. I chased him from the family, he was an empty suit. He did nothing for us but get in the way. He was a babbo, useless. How did he get involved in this murder?"

"He was a roommate of my cousin in the shelter," Angelo continued. "We think whoever came after Rasman found my cousin and thought he was Rasman. But that's all speculation. I did find a vendetta mark on the bathroom door and it had the initials R.R., so I thought about who it could be. You came to mind."

"A vendetta? But my people haven't whacked anyone in years. Why would someone be after us?"

"We hoped maybe you would have an answer," Angelo said.

Wiseguy Murders

"You think someone is after me through Rasman? He doesn't even know where I am. I chased him from the family in New York, and it was months before I came out here."

"Well, we think someone figures that Rasman knows your location. I just wanted to give you a heads up on this," Angelo said.

"Thank you, Angelo, I appreciate that. I'll have my son warn the men." He looked to Antonio and said, "Son, come here."

The man stood and came around the desk to his father. He stopped next to him.

"This is my son Antonio. He takes care of business now that I'm a little slow in moving. Antonio is a good son and takes care of me. He will show you the same respect I give you." He looked up to his son and said, "Go ask Angiola if she has our lunch ready."

"I will, Papa," he said and went out of the room.

"You have to stay for lunch. My Angiola prepares such fantastic dishes. None of these hot dogs or hamburgers, just good Italian foods."

I hope there wasn't anything too spicy, my stomach wasn't in any shape to take that.

Antonio came back to the door and said the food was ready. He went to his father and pulled over a wheelchair and helped the man into it.

As he was being moved, he asked, "Do you have any ideas why these mystery killers would be after me? Any idea who is behind this?" He was rolled out of the library into the hallway towards the dining room.

Angelo looked to me, "Go ahead, Jim."

"Well, sir, we've narrowed the suspects down to Carmine Petrochelli," I said.

Romanny held up his hand and Antonio stopped pushing him. "Carmine is not a Petrochelli. He is a Sambullio. He took Marco Petrochelli's last name when his mother married Marco." He looked to Brigitte. "Did you know this, my child? That he took your good name?"

"No, Uncle. I just assumed when his mother married my dad, his name would be Petrochelli, too," she replied.

"Sambullio doesn't deserve to use the Petrochelli name. My brother and I are at odds and have a problem between us, but I don't like this young Turk trying to get his hands on Marco's family. If anyone wants to get to me, it would be him. He wants my fortune, probably to finance his attempt to become a capo." He finally mentioned the money.

He gave a frown and flicked a thumb off his upper lip. I knew that was like giving the finger. He motioned to his son and whispered into his ear. We couldn't hear him. Antonio nodded his head a couple times and motioned to one of Romanny's lieutenants to take his place pushing Romanny. Antonio went off down the hall and disappeared into a room.

Romanny said to continue to lunch and we entered a big dining hall. The table was set up regally for a simple lunch. The bruiser pushed Romanny to the head of the table, and locked the wheels.

"Let's not let this new development ruin our lunch. It will be taken care of, so enjoy all this good food," he said.

The servants brought out plates of food under covers. They lifted the covers and the food actually looked good. Romanny asked Brigitte if she would give a prayer of thanks and Brigitte did. Her prayer was very nice, a good Italian prayer. Romanny smiled and stabbed a piece of meat from the plate in front of him.

"We don't stand on formality here. I grew up in a boarding house and we had what they called the

boarding house reach for food. You grab it or starve."
He laughed and passed the plate of meat.

Everything was good. Meat and potatoes,
salads and a couple Italian dishes. I wasn't familiar
with the Italian dishes, but they were good. There
was a little talk at the table, mostly Romanny asking
Angelo about his life in Vegas. He asked me about
my cases and I told him a couple harrowing stories
about dirty bombs and viruses being released in the
city. He was impressed.

About an hour later, Antonio came back into
the room and over to Romanny. He was whispering
in the old man's ear. Romanny smiled and said to us.
"I have a lead on Carmine. He's back in Vegas."

*

Chapter 19

"My son will give you the information as to where you can start to find him," Romanny said. "I'm going to keep the family out of this, unless the police can't do something about it. I've stayed under the radar for years, enjoying my retirement. My son will take over when I'm gone, then he can do what he wants with it." He finished and wiped his mouth with the cloth napkin. "Brigitte, Angelo told me over the phone when he explained you were coming, that you lived with a step-brother. That wouldn't be Carmine?"

"I do stay in his house, yes," she replied. "I don't have my own place, my job has been slow and money is tight. I can't afford my own place."

Romanny waved his hand and said, "No, you can come live here. Get away from that criminale. My granddaughter has little contact with other women, other than the service people. It will be good for her. Is this all right with you?"

Brigitte took on a big smile and said, "I'd love that, Uncle. I'd have to get my things."

"I'll send you with two of my men to gather your stuff. They'll also protect you. We can move you today."

She was grinning from ear to ear and said, "I don't have much, just my clothes and a few accessories. It wouldn't take long."

"It will be good to have a young person around the house. Now, finish your lunch and I'll have my men take you there."

Romanny turned to Angelo and asked, "What has Rasman been up to all these years?"

"Jim's police friend, a homicide lieutenant, did a background check and Rasman has been homeless for about five years. He was living in the flood tunnels before they moved into the shelter. Prior to that, he was registered as working at the Luxor Casino as a dealer. They caught him cheating and he was fired. Before that, he had a long record of petty crimes around New York City," Angelo said.

"He was useless, as I remember. Always getting in the way. He was too needy and wanted attention. He was caught skimming the numbers, so I gave him a pass—get lost or be whacked. He disappeared. Last we saw of him was in New York."

"So, he wouldn't have known you were out here?" I asked.

"No way, unless he was spying on us. When did he move here?"

"My friend said he left New York about eight years ago," I said.

"We moved here eight years ago," he said and looked to his son. "He must have followed us. But why didn't he approach us?"

Antonio said, "We had him pegged for being here. He was being watched and was warned to stay away, then he went underground in the tunnels. It was nothing, so we didn't concern you about it."

Romanny was nodding his head, "He needs to be found. If he knows our location, it could compromise us. Antonio, help Jim and his police friends to find Rasman and quickly."

Romanny looked back to the man who wheeled him in, "Carlo, take me to my room." Then he looked back to us. "I'm sorry, but I tire easily now. Antonio will help you. Brigitte, Antonio will have two men take you to get your things. I'll ask my granddaughter to go along to help you." He motioned to the man and he unlocked the wheels and pulled him back. "I'm very glad you came, Angelo and Jim. When we settle this fiasco with Rasman and the people after him, we'll meet again."

He was wheeled out and we stood. Antonio told Brigitte to follow him and said he'd be back.

I looked at Angelo and said, "That went well. He's not such a bad guy."

"He was once feared by many, until his empire fell apart. I'm sure he can still be dangerous, and if not him, then his son. But, we are safe with his blessings."

"Do you think Antonio would try and take over the empire his father had?"

"Anything is possible," Angelo said. "The Romannys were a big Borgata, a crime family. But they saw the end coming from the feds and other crime families, so they pulled up stakes and disappeared. Along with a large sum of money, which was never found. I think it's a good reason for someone to find Romanny and his money."

"He did make mention of his money once. As for how much he still has after buying this palace and funding all his people, hard to tell," I said.

"I've heard it was a fortune, but that was all hearsay. Antonio will have big shoes to fill," Angelo said as Antonio came back in the room.

"I've sent off Brigitte with my daughter and two men to move her here. It will be good for my daughter, she spends too much time running the family business. Sometimes I feel like I'm not needed." He grinned and picked up a piece of pita bread from the table and took a bite.

"May I ask what your family business is?" I asked, hoping I wasn't pushing the subject.

He smiled again, "Nothing illegal. We are real businessmen now. We have an import business down in the south end of the city. We deal with many of the stores in the city and around the state for everything from novelties to clothing. It's a busy business and my daughter has run it well. Maybe Brigitte can become her assistant and lighten her load."

"That would be real nice for her," Angelo said.

"I appreciate your visit to see my father, even if it came with bad news. He has no relatives who visit him and he gets lonely. His half-brother, Marco, would never come to visit. They have a long-standing feud about money that Marco said should have been his. My father put most of the money into the business. Takes a lot of cash to import stuff, what with shipping and buying, it's not cheap. We have about thirty employees who all have to be paid, not counting the people who work here in the compound. All these wiseguys need money to live."

He grinned and took another bite of the bread. Then he frowned. "My father may not live much longer," he said quietly, then paused, "He has cancer and the doctors say he may not see the end of the year. I've been getting the business put in my name to prevent the government from grabbing what they can from him when he passes. Bastards. That's the problem with doing things legally." He smiled again.

"He's lived a long and good life, something to be proud of," Angelo said.

"He's ninety-two, and he has seen a lot in his lifetime. A lot of bad things, too. I'm not like my father. He was old school mafia, I'm not into that and when he is gone, much of this life will go with him. I'll see that his men can all find families elsewhere, but the Romanny family will no longer be a Borgata. We will be fine upstanding members of society." Now he laughed.

Antonio's cell phone rang and he excused himself. He answered, listened, then said, "Carmine, you hurt my daughter and her cousin and I'll see that you are marked for death."

*

Chapter 20

"No, Carmine, you listen to me. You are a dead man. No two ways about it, *dead man*. I will find you and put you down myself," Antonio said loudly.

He didn't put his phone on speaker, I presumed it was not something he did. We couldn't hear what Carmine was saying.

"If you are after the money, it's gone. The business ate it up, and if you believe what Marco says, there was not a fortune in money taken. Marco lies like a Hollywood starlet. So just let the girls go and maybe, just maybe, I'll ignore your sorry ass. Otherwise, your ass is mine." He hung up.

That took balls to do. To tell the man holding your daughter that you weren't going to cooperate, and hang up on him. The phone rang again. He looked at us, frowned, and answered.

He listened and then said, "Celeste, are you all right?"

He paced a short distance, then said, "Where's Carmine?"

I was going crazy not being able to hear both sides of the conversation, so I just imagined what they were saying.

"Where's Carlo and Lou?" he asked. I moved a little closer hoping to hear. He moved away, not realizing I was there. "Put Carmine back on."

He paused and turned to me, putting his hand over the mouth of the phone. "I'm confused. Carmine doesn't want money and he's not saying what he wants." He put the phone back to his ear and listened. "I don't know where he is. He's not my concern just because he used to work for the family."

I figured he was talking about Rasman. Was it Rasman that Carmine wanted and not Romanny? Now I was confused.

"No, Carmine, I will not go find Rasman. You want him so badly, you find him. Now, turn my daughter and her cousin loose or I'll come kick your ass." He listened for a while longer then said, "Fine. I'll forget that you inconvenienced me and my family. Keep out of my sight or I'll mash you." He hung up.

"Bastard. He never wanted my father, he wants just Rasman for some reason. Whatever, I feel sorry for Rasman."

Wiseguy Murders

"Is he turning your daughter loose?" I asked.

"He was never holding her. He was just flexing his muscles for me. Carlo and Lou were protecting the girls. Carmine only had one other man with him, so he wouldn't try anything, but he saw them at the house. Carmine is a wimp, he needs more men to back him up. He was in Bullhead City trying to get a gang together, but seems the men he got were nabbed by the cops."

"Yes, I was there, my partner and I shot two of them. The other two are in custody."

"Good for you. Keeps Carmine at a disadvantage. Celeste is helping Brigitte get her things and will be back soon. I have to get the maids to prepare a room for Brigitte, please excuse me. Don't leave, I'll be right back." He went out, leaving Angelo and me waiting.

"You know, it seems most of the cases I get on are confusing. Too many players and not enough evidence. I need to keep better track of this timeline."

Angelo laughed and said, "I didn't expect the way this turned out either. Seems like mob families are getting soft, not like the old days."

"Well, the Romanny family has gone legit, and Rico Romanny is on his way out. I'm sure Antonio will bring this into the twenty-first century."

I sat on an easy chair and then Angelo sat. We waited.

About ten minutes later, Antonio came back in and said, "Do you want to wait for Brigitte to return so you can say goodbye?"

"I'm sure she'll be busy with her new life here. Just tell her we'll come by again to see how she's doing." Angelo and I stood. "I appreciate your hospitality and I'll be sure to bring my wife to visit with your father."

"He loves to watch her show. It keeps him up to date on things in Vegas, since he doesn't go out much."

He quietly led us back to the front door. The car was waiting for us and Antonio shook our hands. "Thank you for coming and helping to get this straight. Come by any time."

We got in the car, this one didn't have the windows darkened. I guess they trusted us to know where to find them. I guess it was what they called an olive branch.

Angelo was quiet. "I was hoping to find out who murdered my cousin. I guess it was Carmine's men, but I am not fully sure yet. Martin was in the wrong place at the wrong time. I guess I'll have to accept that." He sat looking out the window as we drove. I knew where we were and I could find my way back.

Angelo had pulled his cell phone and called Mario to come and pick us up, so when we arrived he was waiting for us. He stood grinning by Angelo's limo and opened the door of the car we were in.

Angelo slid out and thanked the driver. We went to his car and Mario opened the door. I had to say, Mario was efficient. He drove us back to the restaurant and I went to my car after telling Anglo that I would see him soon.

"Keep me informed about anything you find," he called to me at my car. I waved and nodded.

I drove to the office thinking about my morning. It was a real ride. I was amazed by the turn in the case. Carmine wasn't after Romanny. But the vendetta mark on the door had RR initials under the symbol. Rasman had an R in his name but he was Sal not Ral. I laughed at the thought. I'd have to ask Deacon if Sal had another name. Maybe Rasman had something on Carmine and was a marked man. If we could get to Rasman, we'd maybe find out. But the man was moving too quickly. Especially with Carmine and the cops after him. I'd have to see if anyone still in the tunnels knew of Rasman and if anyone noticed that he went back underground. Not that I wanted to go back in there. Maybe Fred could help.

I arrived at the office and saw Penny's car in the back lot. Willy and Henry were in the big cage, Fred and Buck were sitting on the new picnic table. I parked and went to them.

"Is this the new rest area, what's wrong with the lounge and the A/C?" I asked.

"We decided to get some fresh air, even if it is dusty today. The joys of being in the desert," Buck responded. "Any reaction from the mob head?"

"Well, it was an interesting morning." I sat next to Buck and explained what went on. I finished and said, "So, we are not much further ahead. I have to call Deacon and let him know about what we found out."

Fred said, "It sounds like this Carmine is behind the murder of Scarpo."

"I'd say he was, but we should never assume until we have proof, or some good facts," I said, with a smile.

*

Chapter 21

I left Buck and Fred to go into my office to call Deacon about my morning. I saw Penny down the hall through the glass doors to the lobby. She was talking to Lacey at the counter. I moved into my office quickly to avoid talking to her until I got hold of Deacon. I sat at my desk and pulled my cell phone. I didn't want to use my desk phone, it would light up the button on the desk phone up front. Lacey would know I was in my office. I hit speed dial for Deacon and he came on after a couple rings.

"Jim, I was hoping we wouldn't have to pull you out of Lake Mead with cement around your feet. How did the visit go?"

"Actually, it was very pleasant, until Carmine called," I said, pausing to see what reaction he would give.

"Carmine called. Where is he?"

"He should be back at his house right about now. That was the last place he was reported to be. Now the fun stuff," I said and continued, "Carmine wasn't after Romanny, but he does want Rasman for some reason. So, I'm betting Carmine, or his hoods,

138

had something to do with Scarpo's murder. Romanny has cancer and may not make it to the end of the year, or so his son said. Antonio Romanny is the son and he seems to be a decent guy. They are in the business of importing now, and trying to be legit."

"Hold on while I send some men to pick up Carmine," he said, I could hear him set the phone down. I waited. After a few minutes he came back on.

"Okay, I got men going to pick him up. Now, you say they are going legit in importing? You do know that a number of mob families get into importing to smuggle in drugs and humans for trafficking?"

"I know that, but I don't think they are. But, I could be wrong. Antonio seems okay, I guess we'll just wait and see. Have you turned Romanny's location into OCU?" I asked.

"I wanted to wait until you were in and out before I did. I didn't want OCU to suspect you of getting friendly with Romanny."

"Too late, he and I are old friends now, since he found out I was married to Penny. She's his favorite local show."

"She'll get you into trouble yet," Deacon said with a laugh. "What's Romanny like?"

"He's feeble and needs a wheelchair to get around. He's alert and I'm sure his brain is still sharp. I wouldn't turn my back on him."

"Well, he's been out of circulation for many years, so I don't think we have to worry about him. Now, what is Carmine up to? We haven't had any leads on Rasman. He was staying at Carmine's house, but I doubt he knew that it was Carmine's place and doubt he went back there."

"Actually, he'd be safer with the Romannys. Although Antonio wasn't too fond of him," I said.

"Hold on, Warren needs to tell me something." Deacon took the phone away and I could barely hear what Greg Warren was saying. Deacon finally came back on. "Well, Warren called a couple cars near the house to go pick up anyone there, and the place was empty. This is getting annoying."

I jumped when Penny came to my door. "Deacon, I'll get back to you. I have a problem here." I smiled and hung up. "So, what's up?"

"You snuck in without announcing yourself. That wasn't nice," she said.

"I had to call Deacon before you started to interrogate me."

"Well, I need to know how your morning with the Godfather went?"

"He's no longer a Godfather. He's the boss of a mob family that gave up long ago. They are legitimate now and have an import business."

"Importing drugs?"

"No, novelties and clothing for local businesses. Tourist crap, I guess. But the old man in charge has a special place in his heart for you."

"Me?"

"Yep, I admitted I was married to you and he wants to meet you now. So, you'll have your chance to meet the Godfather."

She got a big smile and said, "I'll get real pretty for him. When do we go?"

"Well, there's a matter of finding a gangster named Carmine, first. We don't know what he's up to and it could be dangerous for you to go anywhere near the Romanny compound. I'll let you know when it's safe."

"You always get me excited, then you throw cold water on me," she said.

Wiseguy Murders

"That's a delightful vision, especially if you're wearing a t-shirt." I sat back and grinned. Luckily, she was too far away to hit me. She made a noise with her tongue and went out.

I stood and went out the back door. Buck and Fred were still relaxing on the picnic table. "You two feel like taking a ride over to the shelter?"

Buck looked at Fred and smiled. "Shall we go bail out the big shot P.I.?"

Fred suppressed a laugh and said, "If you insist. He needs us." They stood and followed me to my car. I called Lacey on my phone and told her where I would be with Buck and Fred. I told her to tell Penny to watch the dogs in the pen. We drove to the shelter and I parked in front. Reverend Harold was standing in the parking lot with two other men. We went to them.

"Harold, how's things here?" I asked.

"Good, Jim. Did you go see Romanny?" he replied.

"I did, how did you know?"

"Deacon was questioning me about the man this morning, asking if I knew him. He mentioned that you were going to see him with Angelo."

"It was a unique opportunity to meet an old-school mafia family. Although, they are a legitimate company now. We found out that a man named Carmine was after Rasman. I presume his people found Scarpo, and either thought he was Rasman or roughed him up to find out where Rasman was. The police are looking for Carmine now." The men with Harold gave their apologies and left us. "Can you gather everyone in the main room, I'd like to talk to them."

"I can do that. Besides, it's lunch time, so everyone should already be there." He turned and went towards the main room. Buck, Fred and I followed.

The room was full of people—men and women. There were a few children with their parents. I asked Harold if he would go ask the parents to take the children out. I was going to be talking about murder, something not suitable for children. He went off and I turned to Fred.

"Fred, how many of these people do you know?" I asked.

"Maybe a dozen or so from the tunnels, the rest came from the streets. I never got to know them."

"Okay, I'd like you to stand by me while I talk," I said.

"Just to give you some cred?" he asked with a smile.

"Something like that. A few of these people know me, you'll help me to be respectable."

Buck was standing by us and said, mostly to himself, "I wouldn't find you respectable."

"Well, thank you, Buck. I'll have you standing by to threaten anyone who doesn't cooperate."

"Now that I can do," he said, showing his walrus grin.

*

Chapter 22

After the children and their families had left the room, I went up front to the podium that Harold used for his sermons. I tapped the microphone and then looked to my crew who were standing by. Buck grinned and said to be respectable. I gave him a quick finger and he laughed.

"May I have your attention, please," I said into the mic. "If everyone could look up here."

I scanned the crowd and waited until they were paying attention. Everyone turned towards the front of the room and went silent.

"Good, thank you. Most of you know me, I'm Jim Richards. You know Buck and Fred," I said pointing to my friends. "We need your help, again. Today, I visited with Rico Romanny and it turns out that the killers weren't after him. We are now looking for Carmine Petrochelli, also known as Carmine Sambullio." That name got a reaction from someone in the group. I moved around the podium and asked, "Someone just made it clear that the name Sambullio is familiar. Who was that?" I went to the edge of the tables and looked around. A couple men were pointing out one man trying to hide his face. I went between the tables, up to the man.

"You know Carmine Sambullio?" I asked him. He glanced sideways at me, and said quietly, "Leave me alone."

I took his arm gently and asked him to come with me. He pulled away and jumped up, running away from me. Buck took giant leaps towards the man before he could get out the door. Buck tackled the man and then pulled him up by his collar. I went up to them and grabbed his arm a little harder.

"Buck, take him to the office. I'll be there shortly." Buck got a good hold on the man and took him out of the community room. I went back to the podium, Fred was still standing there. He had a strange look on his face.

"Fred, are you all right?"

"Sambullio. I know them. I know the family and they are, or were, ruthless. The son murdered his father to take over the family, but the Feds moved in and broke them up before the son could get a grip. I don't know his name, but I'll bet this Carmine is the son."

I was feeling odd now, thinking that this man was very dangerous. I was surprised that Carmine didn't mess with Antonio Romanny. But since the girls had two bodyguards and Carmine was at a disadvantage, I guess he decided not to push the issue. He wanted Rasman and he wasn't interested in the Romannys. Again, I wondered what Rasman was wanted for.

"Fred, how much do you know about the Sambullios?"

"Enough to help your investigation. I looked into a couple families to join after I left Angelo's family. They were breaking up at the time when Angelo's step-father was murdered. No one knew who did it, but it was mentioned that the Sambullios were involved."

"Damn, if Angelo knows or finds out this Carmine was involved, he may go on a vendetta," I said.

"I'm not telling him," Fred responded.

"Good, now come with me and we'll see what our mystery friend knows." I went to the podium and thanked everyone. "If anyone else knows anything about the Sambullio family, please go to the office."

I shut off the microphone and headed to the door. Fred followed me out of the community room and down to the office. We entered, Buck had the man in a chair in the middle of the room. Harold was standing nearby watching it all.

147

Wiseguy Murders

I went to the man after pulling a chair to him. I straddled the chair and looked into his face. His skin was well worn and pocked, probably from acne or beatings. He had a look of having seen too much in his life. "What's your name?" I asked.

He said, "Doug."

"So, Doug, you have knowledge of the Sambullios? What can you tell me?"

The man glanced nervously around the room. I wondered what had him on edge.

I told him, "I'll see that you are protected for sharing your information. We need to stop Carmine and you can help. If we can stop him, you should be safe."

He looked up to me and gave me a dirty, tooth-stained smile. "You think Carmine can be stopped? He's slipped through every attempt to take him down. He's evil and not someone to be fooling with."

"Well, Antonio Romanny took him down a notch today. I'm sure I could get Romanny to protect you in exchange for info on Sambullio."

"I didn't want to say anything, but those two men who came to the parking lot while we were shooting hoops asked for Rasman, I didn't think they were enforcers. I told them which room and they went there. I didn't mean to get Scarpo killed. I was afraid to talk after that."

"When the men asked you about Rasman, what exactly did they say?"

He paused for a moment, his face contorting as he thought back. "They asked if we knew Sal Rasman. I said I knew of him, then they asked where he was. I told them where his room was and they left me. That's all. I didn't think they were going to do harm."

"How well did you know Rasman?"

"I knew him from the tunnels. He told me all about his days working for the Romanny family. I didn't believe him, he was a broke down bum who couldn't possibly have been a made man for the mob. I just listened and let it go. I was wrong, if the Sambullios are after him."

"They're after him with a vengeance. Be glad they don't know you." I turned to Fred. "What do you think Carmine is up to?"

"I have no idea. If Rasman did him wrong, Sambullio would be hard to stop. He was a hard head and didn't forgive easily. I remember hearing about an incident where a man looked a little too long at a woman Sambullio was with at a restaurant, he exploded, claiming that they were fooling around, and beat up both the man and the girl. The police came, but Sambullio had people in high places and he was released the next morning. The man and woman spent a number of days in the hospital. That was back in New York, he's a nobody out here in Vegas, but that doesn't make him any less dangerous."

I turned back to Doug. "Thank you, Doug. I may need you to explain that to a friend of mine. He's a cop, but he's a good guy. We need to take Sambullio down. If the police don't get him, I'm sure the Romanny family would love to. Or my friend Angelo DeMarko."

Doug stared at me. "You're friends with Angelo?"

"Good friends, yes. Why?"

"Angelo is someone who is going places. He's a tough cookie, and I wouldn't mess with him."

Now I wondered about Angelo again. Was he getting his own family started, or just gathering mob rejects to hang with? He had given us a lot of help in the past, volunteering his men for some of my cases. He was good to have around, and had been there all the way back to the Bridezilla killer. Definitely a good friend to have.

Chapter 23

I turned Doug loose after telling him we wouldn't let anyone know that he gave us any info. He skittered out of the office and disappeared. I pulled my cell phone and called Deacon.

Buck, Fred and Harold were sitting around the office as I paced. Deacon finally answered after a couple rings. "Talk to me," he said.

"Got some new info about Carmine. He's actually a Sambullio. Ever hear of that family?"

"I think so, they were a low level mob family out of New York. They fell apart a number of years ago, after the Feds dug into them. So Carmine is a Sambullio."

"An informant told me more about him and also said he's very dangerous. Any word as to where he is?"

"Not yet. I got everyone looking for him. He's laying low. He slipped out of his house but we're watching for him."

Wiseguy Murders

"It turns out I have one resident here who knew Rasman fairly well from the tunnels. He warned us that Carmine was very dangerous, and I think you should be on alert."

"Thanks for the concern. I'll let you know if we find him. Where is this informant?"

"He's still here, do you think we should watch him?"

"Well, do the other residents know he talked to you?"

I thought about that and said, "Hold on." I turned to Buck and said, "Go get Doug and bring him back here." I went back to Deacon, "Can you provide protection for him until we nab Carmine?"

"I'll see what we can do," he replied.

"I'll bring him to you for further questioning." He agreed, we finished and hung up.

I looked at Fred, still standing by, and said, "After we drop Doug off to see Deacon, we'll head back to the office. I don't think we can get much more here." Buck came back with Doug and I explained to him that he could be in danger and I have a friend in the LVPD who wants to talk to him and give him protection. He agreed.

Bob Moats

Buck, Fred and I, along with Doug, went to my car and drove to meet Deacon. I introduced them and Deacon said he'd take care of it from there. I went to my car and drove back to the office.

Penny was in the dog cage with the animals. I parked and went over to her. "I think I'll lock you in there. Leave you out here for a while to get some fresh air."

"You do and you won't be breathing much air." She walked to the gate and came out. "So, anything new in the gangster chase?"

"Nope, everyone is still missing. But Deacon has his men on it. I'm going in to relax in my office. If you'd like to come in and sit on my lap, I won't object." I flashed her a grin.

"I'd rather be in the cage with the dogs," she said, and walked past me to the back door. I looked down at Willy and Henry and laughed. They were sitting next to each other watching me.

I entered my office and sat at the desk, wondering what new adventures would happen. I saw Earl walk past my door and Trapper was behind him. I hadn't seen Trapper since we investigated the Santa murders. I stood and went out to see them go into Earl's office. I went to the door and looked in. They were looking at some maps as I entered. Trapper noticed me first.

"Hey, Jim. Where have you been hiding?" he asked.

"I was visiting a mob family. The Romannys."

Earl gave me a strange look and said, "You actually visited with Rico Romanny? Where?"

"Right here in Vegas. Why, and how do you know Rico?"

"You're on a first name basis now? How nice. He was, at one time, a big shooter in the Mafioso. Feared by many, then he just up and vanished. Where did you visit with him?"

"As I said, here in Vegas. He has a compound out by Summerlin. He's old and feeble now, his son is more in charge. They went legit, importing tourist crap to stores now."

Earl laughed. "I can imagine what they're importing."

"I didn't question them about it. But I had a nice visit. I think the old man is friendly," I said.

"You took Angelo with you, right?" Trapper asked.

Bob Moats

"He was the one who got us in," I replied

"Angelo has enough mob blood in his veins that even Romanny would fear him."

"I keep getting this vibe that Angelo is getting back into the family business."

"He knows enough people to start one. Vegas may no longer be a foot hold for the mobs, but there are a good number of them left around the city," Earl said.

"I guess I'll have to have a talk with him," I said.

"Sure, he may make you one of his lieutenants," Earl said with a laugh.

"I'm not interested in joining any mob family, even Angelo's. So, what are you two up to?"

"We are plotting a vacation with the women. Somewhere out in Denver," Trapper replied.

"Who's going to take care of Deacon and Lynn's baby if Paula is going with you?" I asked Earl.

"Lynn found a nice little old lady in her apartment building who will watch the kid. I'm hoping she continues to watch, so Paula won't be getting too maternal. I'm not ready for a family," he said with a laugh.

"You're too old for a family. Besides, I don't think your children would be interested in learning all your black-ops talents," I said. "Both of you are too old to settle down," I laughed at the thought of Trapper changing diapers and told him so.

"I could change diapers if need be. Hopefully, it will never be needed," he replied.

"So, are you still trying to solve the murder of Angelo's cousin?" Earl asked.

"We pretty much figured it was a gangster named Carmine Sambullio who sent men to do the job."

"Sambullio?" Earl said and gave me a concerned look. "You really are delving into the underworld, aren't you? Do you know much about the Sambullios?"

"No," I replied.

"I'll just say, beware," Earl said ominously. "Carmine was reputed to have murdered his own father to take over the family. But the Feds got into Carmine's face and he disappeared. Have you called the Feds in on this?"

I thought about that, and maybe I should have a talk with Deacon about it. At least have him talk to Organized Crime to see what they have on Carmine. "Maybe I'll suggest it to Deacon. Now don't go tearing Denver apart, leave some for the tourists."

I left them to plot mass destruction, and went up to the front to see what the women were plotting. I saw Lynn at the counter and went through the glass doors.

"Jim, we were just talking about you," Lynn said. Penny was sitting next to Lacey's desk and Lacey was relaxing in her chair.

"Strange, my ears weren't buzzing. What did I do now?" I asked.

"We were thinking about calling you the Godfather of Richards Investigations."

I just stared in wonder. "Why is everyone putting me in a mob lately?" I asked.

*

Chapter 24

"Maybe you should start your own little crime family. Deacon can be a corrupt cop on the take and Penny could be your gun moll," Lynn said with a laugh.

"I like that," Penny said. "My gun is always ready to shoot."

"Well, you'll have to do without me. I've had enough mob involvement to last a while. I'm going to meditate, so stay out of my office." I turned and went back through the glass doors and down to my office. I thought about keeping the door open, but that would just invite pests. I closed it.

I was just starting to relax when my cell phone buzzed. I forgot to shut it off. I answered after seeing it was Deacon. "Is this important?" I asked.

"It is if you want to hear about Rasman," he replied.

I sat straight up in my chair and woke up. "You have him in custody?"

"Well, let's say he's not going anywhere. He's in the morgue."

Now that really woke me up. "When, how?"

"Patrol found his body about an hour ago on the side of a road. He was dumped from a moving vehicle, Joe Lang reported, judging from the position of his body and scuff marks on his face. Not a very ceremonious way to go. Joe said he was murdered execution style, shot in the head from behind and above. Rasman had to have been on his knees or seated."

"Damn, now we won't find out anything from him. Nothing to tie anyone to his killing?"

"Nope, I still have a watch out for Carmine. He's our only connection to Rasman, now. If Carmine did get hold of Rasman, then he may have the info that Rasman had."

"If Rasman talked. Then again, maybe Carmine just wanted to execute Rasman . Maybe Rasman didn't have any information and Carmine just had a need to murder him," I said. "I was thinking about the body that was dumped at the shelter. Did you get any info on him?"

I heard papers being shuffled around then Deacon said, "He was Herman Franklin, a banking officer at Bank of America. No idea how he ties into this unless he was in the wrong place at the wrong time."

"What kind of banking officer was he?"

"A branch manager. What are you thinking?" Deacon asked.

"Maybe he had something that Carmine wanted, too. But they couldn't get Franklin to talk. Or maybe he did talk, so they needed Rasman to complete the puzzle. Franklin's body was dumped at the shelter to show Rasman that they were on his trail."

"You're really talking yourself into a box aren't you?"

"At least I'm thinking."

"I'll give you that."

"What branch did Franklin work at?" I asked.

"The one on Maryland, by the UNLV campus. Are you thinking of going there?"

"It's better than sitting around." I replied.

"Jim, it's getting late and you've had a busy day. Besides, the bank is closing soon, most of the workers would rather go home than talk to you."

I looked at my watch and agreed. "I'm going first thing in the morning, if you can break away."

"I'll be at your office at eight, don't be late." He hung up before I could say I don't get out of bed before eight. Oh well, I'll have to make an exception.

I found Penny in the lounge playing pinball. Lynn was watching her and turned to me. "You shouldn't have gotten this thing. We spend too many quarters in it."

"Those quarters go to buy you guys coffee and donuts, so suck it up." I went up behind Penny and poked her in the sides. She jumped, lost the ball and turned to hit me. I ran to the door and said I was going home.

I hollered at Lacey to lock up and go home as I ducked out of the door, then I went to my car and drove out.

Penny and I were relaxing after we made and ate dinner and then she started yawning. "I get it, time for bed," I said, and got up from the couch, helping her up. We retired to the bedroom and Willy jumped up on his *Bates Motel* chair that we kept in the room since he liked it. A half hour later we were asleep.

Wiseguy Murders

I had set my alarm to get up in plenty of time to be at the office by eight. I thought about making Deacon wait for me, but he'd just bother Lynn and I didn't want to get her upset with me. Penny was in her bathroom and I yelled to the door that I was leaving. She yelled something back, but I couldn't understand her with the water running, so I headed out.

I went in the back door of the office, no one was around. I saw Fred in the lobby through the glass doors, he was vacuuming. I looked at my watch and discovered it was seven and not eight. How did I do that? Penny must have known it was earlier than we usually leave. Maybe she was yelling that through the bathroom door. I just couldn't hear her with the water running.

"Hey, Fred," I said, as I came into the lobby. He looked surprised when he heard me. "Sorry, I hope I didn't frighten you?"

"No, not fright, just surprised that you are here so early."

"Don't ask, because I don't know how I managed to do this either. I'll be in my office if you need me." I went back through the doors to my office. I sat at my desk wondering what to do. I fired up my computer and worked on my latest book until I heard the front lobby door open. Lacey came to my door.

"Everything okay at home? You didn't have a fight with Penny, did you? You better not have made Penny mad at you," she said.

"No, we didn't have a fight." I thought about that, Penny and I never fought. We discussed things, but never had an argument in all the time we were together. No reason to, we always agreed on things. "I came in early to get some work done."

She stared at me, unbelieving, "You keep telling yourself that." She turned and went off.

I wondered how I could ever do without her. She was a smart-ass, but it was the way she did it. She was funny. In the almost three years since Lacey jumped off the Stratosphere tower, somehow lived, and we cleared her of murder charges, she had become a part of our family.

My cell phone buzzed and the display said that Deacon was calling. I looked at my watch, it was just before eight. "You better not be telling me that you aren't coming in. I've been here since seven, waiting."

I heard him laugh. "No, I'll be there shortly. I did a little digging and got a warrant to check the bank's customer database to see if Rasman ever had an account there."

"Does that warrant extend to opening up a safety deposit box?" I asked.

"I made sure it did. I just called to make sure you were in. See you shortly." He hung up and I sat back. I was hoping we would find a link between the banker and Rasman.

*

Chapter 25

About ten minutes later, Deacon came through my door and stood waiting. "Well, good morning sunshine," I said.

"It's already hot outside and I'm not crazy about being up early anymore. I didn't sleep well, the baby is still doing her best to see that I don't sleep. Are you ready to go to the bank?"

I didn't want to further the comments about sleep or babies, so I stood and we went out. "I can drive if you want to sleep on the way," I offered.

He grumbled something I couldn't hear as we passed Lacey in the hall. I told her I was going to be gone for a while and she mumbled something I couldn't hear. I probably needed my hearing checked.

Once outside, Deacon said we'd take the unmarked car, since it was official business. I think he just liked driving the Charger. We got in and drove over to Maryland Parkway just below Flamingo Road, and into the bank parking lot. We got out and went in, finding the place unusually quiet. We went over to the area were the bank officers were and Deacon asked where we could find the person in charge.

The woman looked sad and said, "Since the death of Mr. Franklin, I was put in charge. May I help you?"

Deacon showed his badge and said, "And you are?"

"Virginia Hayes."

"Well, Virginia, I have a warrant to search your customer database for one particular person. Can you do that?"

Now she smiled, much better than the frown. "Yes, I can. May I see the warrant first?" Deacon handed it to her. She glanced it over then asked, "What is the person's name you wish to find?"

"Try Salvatore Rasman and see if that pops up."

She turned to her computer and started to type. She hit a few more buttons and said, "Yes, we do, as a matter of fact. Although he doesn't have an account with us, he does have a safety deposit box."

Deacon and I looked at each other and grinned. Finally, something tangible. "May we get into the box, my warrant covers that also."

"No problem. Do you have his key?" she replied happily.

Deacon grumbled again. "I don't have a key. Mr. Rasman was murdered and left nothing on his person."

"Oh dear, that could be a problem. We'd need a key to open his box."

"Maybe that's what Carmine was after from Rasman. The key," I said to Deacon. I looked at the woman and asked, "How do you get in the boxes if someone loses their key?"

"We have a locksmith who can open the box and replace it with a new lock."

"How long would it take to get your locksmith out here to open Mr. Rasman's box?" Deacon asked.

"I can call. They usually come out quickly."

"Do that. We have to get in the box. Thank you." Deacon turned to me, "This is going to be a long day, I can feel it."

The woman made the call and then finished. "He said he would be here shortly. Who is going to pay for the locksmith call?"

That threw Deacon. "Uh, I didn't know we'd have to pay for it."

"Someone has to, and since you are requesting the call, then the police should pay for it."

"I'll take care of it," I told Deacon and the woman.

"Fine, you can settle with the locksmith," she replied.

We wandered around the bank for about ten minutes, then noticed a grubby looking man with a large black satchel lumbering in through the door. We figured it was the guy we were waiting for, so we went to him.

Wiseguy Murders

"Are you the locksmith?" Deacon asked, showing his badge.

"That be me, whatcha got?" he said with a toothy smile.

"Safety deposit box," Deacon answered.

"Ah, simple job. Take me to it."

We went back to Virginia and she smiled at the man. "Hello Mr. Winthrop. How are you today?"

"Fine, Virginia. I was on a call nearby and they told me to come here."

Virginia stood and led us to the vault where the boxes were located. We entered and she read from a slip of paper that indicated which box to open. The man pulled out a big drill from his bag and plugged it into the nearest outlet. We watched as he proceeded to drill and do his best to open the door to the box. After about ten minutes he had the door open.

He was putting his equipment back after installing a new lock and I asked how much. He told me and I paid him, asking for a receipt. Just to have the LVPD reimburse me.

Virginia pulled the rather large box from its hole and gave it to Deacon. She then led us to a private room to examine the contents. "I'll be right outside when you are done." She closed the door and we opened the top of the box.

Inside was an envelope and something wrapped in a cloth. Deacon took exam gloves out of his pocket and put them on. He handed me a pair and I pulled them on. He carefully removed the envelope, lifting it carefully to peek under it. I presumed for a booby trap. He found none. He opened the envelope and removed a piece of paper.

He read aloud, "To whoever reads this, I must be dead. The gun with this letter is the murder weapon that Carmine Sambullio used to kill his old man. It should have his prints on it and the bullets should match. I was with Sambullio and two other men when he went to murder his old man and his wiseguys. There were three of them, and Sambullio shot them all. He tossed me the gun and told me to dump it in the river. I didn't. I kept it in case he ever tried anything against me. He later murdered the other two men that were with us and I slipped away and came to Vegas to hide out. I hope Carmine rots in prison. Signed, Salvatore Rasman."

"Well, this clears up a number of things. Carmine didn't want the Romannys, he just wanted Rasman for this," I said. "Now you have the murder weapon, I'm sure Federal Organized Crime would love to have it."

Wiseguy Murders

Deacon pulled two evidence bags from his pocket and put the gun and the letter in and sealed them. He put the bags in his coat pocket.

"Yeah, but we need Carmine more, now. Let's get out of here," he said. "This place gives me the creeps."

"Don't like small rooms?" I asked.

"No, Carmine has the key, so he may be coming here to get into the box. I have to get some people watching the place."

"Good idea, I don't want to face him this early in the morning."

We went out and gave the box to Virginia and said no one would be needing it further. She took it and said, "I hope you found what you were looking for."

We were heading out and got to the car when a large van pulled up and out sprang five men with masks and automatic weapons. We ducked behind the police car and watched. The men ran up to the door as Deacon was calling for backup on his cell phone. After he placed the call, he stood.

"I'm going back in. I may be able to do something." He put the murder weapon in the car and went to the front door. I figured he'd need backup, so

I followed him. I also figured I'd get shot, I hoped my life insurance was paid up. Penny was going to be a very rich woman.

Chapter 26

We re-entered the bank and a masked man put a gun in our faces and told us to go to the side and get on the ground. We did. From our position on the floor, I was watching Virginia, who was having a panic attack explaining to one man that the police took the contents of that box.

He spun around and screamed, "Damn the cops! Now they have it. I'm screwed." He went towards the door and yelled, "Move out! We got to get organized and regroup from this."

Just as they got to the door, a number of patrol cars came barreling up. The men started shooting at the cars. Deacon and I jumped up from our position on the floor and ducked behind a counter, aiming our weapons at the men. We shouted at them to freeze and they turned their guns towards us. We had no choice but to fire.. Deacon took out three of them, while I took out one. It was enough to get the man who seemed to be the leader to surrender. I kept my gun on him while Deacon carefully went to the window to signal all was good. The men outside recognized Deacon and came running up and into the building. The customers in the lobby were still on the floor terrified, and weren't about to move.

"Well, that didn't last long, did it?" I said to Deacon.

"The way I like them," Deacon said, and pulled the mask from the man. "Well, I've only seen one photo of Carmine Sambullio, but I would swear this was him."

"Screw you, cop," he spit out. Deacon was going to turn him over to the patrol cops, but decided he wanted the honors of bringing in a notorious gangster and said so.

"Better believe I'm notorious," Sambullio said loudly.

One of the patrol cops behind Sambullio said, "Who is this guy?"

Sambullio spun around and said, "I took over one of the biggest crime families in New York, you flatfoot."

"Yeah, by murdering your own father," I said.

Bob Moats

He glared at me, but said nothing. I grinned as Deacon cuffed the man. We took him out to the Charger, leaving the rest of the men to take care of the crime scene. Joe Lang crossed our path in the parking lot and stopped to complain about the number of bodies at the scene.

"Why can't you just wound them?" he said. "Then it would be LV Medical's problem. I got bodies piling up."

"Sorry, Joe. I'll remember that during the next big shoot out," Deacon said as he pushed Sambullio into the car. "I guess it got the better of me."

Joe went off to take charge of the dead, as we hauled Sambullio to the precinct. We were driving up Maryland towards Flamingo when I was looking at Deacon to say something and noticed out of the corner of my eye that Sambullio was not in the back seat. I looked back and saw he was on the floor.

I yelled, "Ambush!" just as a van pulled up alongside the driver's side of our car, and the van's sliding door opened. A man leaned out and started firing an automatic weapon. Deacon's side window shattered from the bullets, spraying safety glass across us. I ducked forward to avoid being shot. Deacon must have steered towards the van because I felt a huge bump and heard a scraping noise. The Charger lurched to the left again and I felt another bang. I hoped Deacon was alright as he hit the

173

brakes. The car stopped and I came up with my Glock in hand. I saw the van had crossed the road and run head-on into a huge delivery truck. The van crumpled and the shooter fell out onto the road to be struck by a car trying to swerve out of the way of the accident.

I looked to Deacon, he was bleeding from the head. "Shit," I yelled and pulled my cell phone and called 911. I got out of the car and ran to the van, it was pretty much destroyed. The driver of the truck came running out and screamed, "I couldn't avoid them, they crossed the road."

I hurried back to Deacon, he looked unconscious. I opened his door and held him up to keep him from falling out. I closed his door again and looked in the back seat. Sambullio was still on the floor. I pulled open the back door and grabbed him. I pulled him out of the car and put my Glock to his head.

"If my friend dies, I'll claim you were trying to escape and I shot you, you son of a bitch. Who the hell do you think you are? You anachronistic waste of life." A few seconds later, two patrol cars rolled up and the officers got out, running to us. Both of them had medical training and took Deacon out of the car, carefully. About two minutes later, the EMS screamed up and the med techs jumped out running to Deacon. The road was blocked off by the patrol officers and they put Deacon on a gurney and got him in the EMS unit. I asked if he was alive, they said just barely, but they would do what they could.

Gregg Warren came running up since he heard the radio report. "Jim, what the hell happened?"

I told him, and said to take the scum, Sambullio, into custody. Warren and two officers pulled Sambullio up and dragged him to a waiting car. I yelled to Warren to be cautious with him. Warren gave them directions and the two cars drove out with him. I went to the van just as Joe Lang drove up.

"How's Deacon? I heard over the radio."

"I don't know. They took him to LV Medical. He didn't look good." I was upset. "I got to call Lynn to let her know." Joe went off to take charge of the bodies of the men in the van. There were just two, the driver and the shooter.

I went and sat on the curb and speed dialed Lynn on my phone. She came on after three rings. "Hey, Jim, what's up?"

"I got some bad news," I said and told her what happened and then said they were taking Deacon to LV Medical. I heard her hang up, I didn't blame her.

Wiseguy Murders

I sat looking at the Charger riddled with bullets. Too bad some didn't reach Sambullio. Then I looked over to the van. It was a mess. They had to extract the driver, he was dead. Good.

I stood, went to Greg Warren and asked if he could give me a ride to the hospital. He agreed and we left.

About ten minutes later, with Warren using his sirens and lights, we arrived at the hospital. He pulled up to the ER entrance where ambulances and police parked. We got out and went in. I asked the ER nurse at the desk where Detective DeAngelo was. Warren showed his badge and asked also. The woman checked her record and told us where to go. We went into a waiting room where we found Lynn with Penny.

Penny came to me and said, "You didn't get shot, did you?"

I looked down at my body and said, "No."

"Good, because if you did, I would murder you." She patted my stomach and went back to Lynn.

*

Chapter 27

I went over to Lynn. She didn't look well and had been crying. She looked up to me and said, "I know that being a cop means you can get shot. I just never figured Deacon would. This is a rude awakening. What happened, Jim?"

I sat next to her and explained the circumstances of the situation. She sat listening and nodding as I talked. "Best I can figure is the second van must have been watching from across the street and saw us take Sambullio to Deacon's car. Then they followed us. They must have had a plan in place for an event like this. Sambullio dropped down to the floorboards, the driver in the van had to have seen him do that. Then it was a simple matter of stopping the car by firing on it, ramming it and getting Sambullio out. Even with being shot at, Deacon thought enough to run the van off the road and stop them. He's a good cop."

She sat looking straight ahead, not saying anything. "This is all your fault," she finally said to me. I cringed and waited for it. "If you hadn't brought Deacon out here from Michigan, we would have never met." She broke a small smile.

177

Wiseguy Murders

I smiled back and said, "Sure, and you would have never married him and had a wonderful daughter. By the way, where is she?"

"There's a woman in our building who agreed to watch her. Paula and Earl are going on vacation."

A door opened and a doctor in scrubs walked in. His scrubs had blood on them. I thought it would have been better if he changed. Lynn stood as he went to her.

"Mrs. DeAngelo, we'll know more in the next few hours. He came through the surgery fine. He sustained three bullet wounds. Two passed through his neck with no damage, but the third lodged in his skull behind his left ear. We'll have to wait and see if there has been any permanent damage, but so far everything looks good. I don't usually joke about these things, but your husband must have a hard head to have survived."

Lynn broke out laughing and sobbing at the same time. "Yes, I tell him he has a hard head all the time, and now he proved it. Thank you, Doctor. When will we know something?"

"As I said, he's resting and we'll give him a couple hours sleep. He should be fine. Don't worry." He turned and went back through the door.

Penny had her arm around Lynn and pulled her back to the couch. They sat while I stayed standing. Warren came back from parking the car in a more legal spot. "Anything?" he asked. I told him what the doctor said. He went and sat on an easy chair looking miserable. With Deacon on the injured list, that meant Greg was next to head up the squad. He wasn't fond of that. I remembered the last time he was in charge. I worked with him and we managed to solve the case.

For the next two hours, we had a number of officers and detectives stopping by to see what was happening. After a while, the waiting room was full of police until Captain Weber came in. I've never seen a group of cops move so fast. Weber didn't even care.

He came to me, "Richards, talk to me. What went down?"

I explained the situation for the umpteenth time and he listened. I finished and he was quiet. That worried me.

"What's his condition?" he asked.

"We're waiting for word. The last the doctor said, he was all right, but they're watching him," I said. "What's the status on Sambullio?"

"He's cooling in a cell. What was it that Deacon wanted him for?"

"Murder of two homeless men, murder of a bank manager and murder of his own father. Plus a number of Federal charges, I'm sure." I reached into my jacket pocket and took out the evidence bags with the gun and letter. I had picked them up while the EMTs were taking care of Deacon. "This is the gun that Sambullio used to murder his father, a New York mob boss named Guillermo Sambullio. I'll go over the details with you later, after we find out about Deacon."

"Good work, Richards," he said, taking the bags and placing them in his jacket pocket.

"Deacon worked hard on this, give him the credit."

"I'll see he gets it," Weber said quietly.

The door opened again and a nurse came in. "Mr. DeAngelo was moved to a private room and he can have visitors briefly. The doctor said he's doing fine."

Weber barked, "That's Detective Lieutenant DeAngelo, Nurse."

She smiled and said, "Sorry, Detective Lieutenant DeAngelo is in a private room and can have brief visitation. He's in room 234." She turned and went out.

Weber turned to Lynn, "Get moving!"

She smiled and went out of the waiting room with us in tow. I saw her ask a nurse where the room was and she got directions. We went to an elevator and up to the second floor, then to the room. We entered and Lynn went right for him, then she stood by his bed. Weber went around the other side and leaned over looking into his face. Deacon had his eyes closed and then slowly opened them. The first face he saw was Weber. "Oh God, I'm in hell," he said groggily. Everyone laughed, including Weber. Deacon turned his head and saw Lynn. She took his hand and then kissed him on the forehead. His head and neck were bandaged up.

"You pull this stunt again and I'll divorce you," she said.

"I'll try not to." He looked at me and asked, "Is Sambullio in custody, we didn't lose him, did we?"

"He's locked up safely. I gave the gun to Captain Weber. It should be enough to prosecute Sambullio. According to Warren, two of the men from the bank attack had lived. I'm sure they'll get a confession from them. Warren can fill you in on all this when you're feeling better."

Wiseguy Murders

"The doctor said if it wasn't for your hard head, the bullet would have done you in. I always knew you had a thick skull," Lynn said with a grin.

"I guess I'll never hear the end of that." He coughed hard a couple times and winced. I imagined his head must have been throbbing.

Weber ordered everyone to get out, except Lynn. "Deacon needs to rest," he barked. We said our goodbyes and went out. Outside the room, Warren was stopped by Weber and I could see he was nervous.

"Greg, we need to talk about this." He looked to me. "Richards, I'll need you, too. I feel you had a hand in this from the start. We can meet in my office in an hour." He turned and went off.

I looked at Warren, "I guess we'll go and listen to him talk?" He nodded. "I'll meet you there." Warren went off. I turned to Penny.

"How did you and Lynn get here?" I asked.

"I drove her over, she wasn't in any shape to drive. I'll wait here with her until she's finished."

"Good, I'll call later to see how it's going." I gave her a kiss on the lips.

She grabbed my jacket lapels. "I'm glad I'm not visiting you here, or in the morgue. You'd better watch more closely in the future." Then she gave me a thorough tonsil search. We broke it up when the elevator door opened and a nurse got off. I stepped in and watched Penny as the door closed.

I got to the ground floor and came out just as I saw Buck coming in the front entrance. "Jim, how's Deacon?"

I repeated the story once more. Maybe I'd write it down for everyone.

*

Chapter 28

I sat in Weber's office explaining what happened from the beginning when they found Scarpo's body in the shelter. I remembered the whole tale, which was good, because it would make a great book. I'd have to start on it this week.

"Good going. I'll see Deacon gets a commendation for his part. Greg," he said to Warren, "you need to get with the Feds to see what all they have on Sambullio. Maybe we can turn this over to them. I put the gun in evidence in case they need it. Sounds like everyone did a fine job. The way I like it. Now, get out of my office, I have work to do."

Warren and I stood and exited his office. I think Greg was relieved that he wasn't asked a lot of questions. He turned to me and said, "I'll go get on the phone with the Federal Task Force for Organized Crime, and see what they can do. If we can get Sambullio transferred to them, it will be easier for us."

"We still have the murder of Martin Scarpo, Sal Rasman and the bank manager. But, I'm sure it will be included in charges against him. Even though

184

he didn't do the hits personally. I got some things to take care of myself, so have fun." I left Warren in the squad room and went to my car. Buck was standing near his car and smiled when I came up. "You know you can come in the precinct," I said.

"Hard to break old habits. I like to stay away from police stations," he replied.

"I'm going over to visit Angelo to tell him what we found. I'll meet you back at the office." He agreed and I went to my car and drove out.

I arrived at the restaurant and parked. I was told Angelo was in the kitchen when I came in. He came out shortly after. He grinned when he saw me.

"Mr. R, what brings you here by yourself? Is Mrs. R all right?"

"She's fine. I have a lot to tell you, so do you have time to talk?"

"Sure do, let's go in my office." I followed him through the kitchen and into his office. We sat.

"So, I just left the hospital where Deacon is resting from being wounded in a gun fight with Sambullio's men. He's fine."

Wiseguy Murders

That got a rise out of Angelo. I went on to explain everything that happened. He sat quietly listening.

"I talked to Detective Greg Warren at the hospital and he said that a couple other detectives interrogated the two survivors from the bank hit and they confessed that Sambullio sent men looking for Rasman, but found your cousin. You know what happened there. They also confessed to killing Rasman and a bank manager. Sambullio is also going to face federal charges for the murder of his father. We have the smoking gun, as they say." I watched Angelo's expressions. He just sat listening and nodding his head.

"I knew you would solve this," he said. "I'd like to deal with Sambullio the old way of the family, but I don't do that anymore."

I just had to ask something that had been on my mind for a couple months now, something I thought about since the Santa murder case. "Angelo, we're friends, so I hope I can ask you this without offending."

"You can ask anything, you know my life as well as I do."

"You've had a number of men help with a couple cases in the past. I never asked where they came from. What I'm wondering is, are you starting your own family out here?"

He gave me a big grin. "Thank you for thinking I could do that. I'm not interested in the affairs of running a crime family. What has been going on is there are a good number of wiseguys still hanging around Vegas. Mostly enforcers from families that fell apart. They took odd jobs and hid under the radar from their past. I started to get with them in social settings. We meet once a month in the banquet room and talk about our adventures. We're not plotting to get into illegal doings, just a bunch of guys talking."

"Does Fred know about this?" I asked.

"Sure, he's been to our first two meetings. You can come to meet them. They are a good bunch of guys when you get to know them."

"I'll do that. Sounds interesting. Maybe I can write books based on their experiences."

"I'm sure they'd love that. Make them immortal like all the big wigs of crime." Angelo laughed out loud. He settled and got serious, "Where's Sambullio now?"

"Locked up. Until the Feds come and get him."

Wiseguy Murders

"I hope he makes it safely," Angelo said with a funny smile. I hoped he wasn't plotting something. But, he explained he wasn't going into the crime family business, so I'd have to assume he was just wishfully thinking. I hoped.

We finished up and I said I had to go check on how Deacon was doing.

Angelo said, "When he's well enough, bring him for a dinner. He deserves it."

I said I'd tell him and went out to my car. I was worn down from the long day and wanted to meditate for the rest of it. I figured that I should check in at the office so drove there. I could call Penny and see how Deacon was doing.

I drove up and Fred was outside working on the flowers with his dog Henry beside him. "Hello, Jim. Buck said you caught Sambullio, but Deacon was hurt."

"Yes, on both counts. I'll explain everything to you later. I want to get to my office and make a few phone calls. Or go play pinball to relax, I don't know yet." I said I'd talk later and went to the building.

I went through the back door and saw Buck, Earl and Trapper in the hallway. "I thought you were going on vacation?"

"We heard about Deacon and waited. What happened?" Earl asked.

I was now sick of telling the story, so I said, "Read about it in my next book." I laughed and headed to the front. I stopped and turned, "He's in room 234 if you want to visit." Then I went through the lobby doors.

"How's Deacon?" Lacey asked.

"He's fine. He'll live to fight another day," I said, just as the front door opened and in came Antonio Romanny. I was surprised. "Welcome. What brings you to my humble office?"

"My father heard about Sambullio, word travels fast with us. He also heard about your police friend and he said that any medical expenses would be taken care of by our company, since Sambullio caused all this trouble." He gave me a smile, "And, he said to remind you to bring your wife out for a visit."

"Tell your father he is a generous man. I'll pass the information. Thank you. How's Brigitte doing?"

"She's having a ball. She and my daughter are getting along fine. It's good that you brought her with you. It's nice to hear laughter around the house."

189

"I'm glad. I was thinking of going into our lounge to take my frustrations of this day out on pinball, care to join me?"

He smiled and said, "I'd love to."

I told Lacey to hold my calls. She just stuck her tongue out at me.

*

Chapter 29

Deacon spent another week in the hospital before they finally let him out. Mostly because he kept complaining. Weber told Deacon to take another week to recuperate and to relax. Deacon was pleased that they gave him a citation for his part in the take down of Sambullio in the bank. I didn't complain that I was part of that, I was just happy for Deacon.

The shelter was back to normal. Mac had his guards take some extra training classes to better learn how to watch for signs of trouble. Buck was off on a case of stolen jewels from some society babe. So, he was happy. Trapper and Earl finally went on vacation after they were sure Deacon was better. They spent a good number of days visiting him, until he told them to stay away. They could get on a person's nerves.

The office was quiet, only Lacey, Lynn and Fred were in the building.

I had talked to Fred about the gangster social club that Angelo had formed. He said they were all a good bunch of guys and had lots of stories to tell. I asked when the next meeting was, and said I might visit. He told me and said we could go together. I liked that, and told him so.

I was in my office relaxing and working on the book about my adventures with the mobs and Sambullio. It was nice to have good stories to write about.

I heard the hallway door from the lobby open and close and wondered who was going to come by. I was surprised when I saw it was Deacon. He had smaller bandages on his wounds now that they took off the wrappings that made him look like a mummy. He smiled and asked if I was busy.

"I'm never too busy for you. Come in and sit," I said standing.

He went to my client chair and sat as I did. "What's up? Feeling the pressure of wanting to get back to work?"

"That's just it. I'm not." He went quiet and was looking like he was trying to find words to say. I waited.

"Jim, when that van pulled alongside and started shooting, I saw the glass shatter and the flash from the automatic aimed at my head. I felt the two bullets hit my neck and I started to pass out when the one hit my head. But not before I started to run them off the road." He paused again, then said, "Jim, while I was passing out, I saw Lynn and our daughter and I didn't want to die. It was not a nice feeling."

"I understand." I said. "I was shot and almost died out in New York. Spent three days in the hospital in a mild coma. I had bad dreams. Not a pleasant experience."

"In my nightly dreams now, I keep seeing my daughter growing up without me. I didn't think I could ever dream that. I started to think this morning, maybe it was a warning. Maybe I should move on to something else other than being a cop and facing gunfire at any time."

"What would you do? As long as I have known you, you've been a cop."

"Lynn made a change. She joined your firm and is out of harm's way now. Do you think you could take on one more investigator?" He looked a bit sheepish. I knew it must be hard for him to ask. It didn't bother me in the least.

"It would give you more time to be with your daughter and Lynn. You could work as needed, like Lynn does. It would be real boring at times, like watching spouses cheat. Have you talked to Lynn about this?"

"No, I'm still up in the air about it. I want to be sure before I commit to it. She did mention the other day about me getting into another line of work. She was kidding, but I think she was secretly serious. What do you think?"

"Deacon, I can't speak for you or Lynn. It's something you two should talk about. I will be more than happy to bring you into the firm. You would be an asset and we are busy enough now to handle an extra person. We've had to turn away clients because we can only handle so much. But with you here and not on LVPD, it may get boring since we'll have less access to good murder cases."

"I'm sure Warren will need our help. He's a great detective, just needs more confidence."

"You talk to Lynn and I'm fine with you joining us." I said just as Lynn came to the door.

"Were you talking about me?" she asked.

I looked at Deacon and said, "You two may as well talk about it." I stood and went to Lynn. "Come on in, you two need to talk." I gently pulled her in and went out, closing the door. I mumbled to myself, "Great, now we need another office."

I went up to the front lobby where Lacey was talking to Willy on her desk. I keep thinking that animals understood her. She smiled when she saw me come in. "I was just telling Willy about how we may have another P.I. working for us."

"Were you spying on my office?"

"Nope, I just had that feeling. Deacon looked like he wanted a change in his life."

"Now you're psychic?"

"A little. It's how I stay ahead of you. So, is he coming on board with us?"

"Don't know yet. He's talking to Lynn."

"Want to listen in? I know how to."

"You better not be listening in my office."

She gave me a big smile just as I saw Lynn and Deacon coming out of my office. "Too late, they're done talking," I told Lacey.

They came through the glass doors from the hallway and Lynn had a very big smile. I was hoping that was a good sign.

Deacon spoke first. "Okay, if you want me and if you can fit me in, I'm fine with joining your firm."

"Weber isn't going to like this," I said with a grin.

Wiseguy Murders

"He'll get over it. So, am I a member of the family?"

"Okay, but you may have to share an office with your wife. I'm not building anymore additions," I said.

"He can set up an office in the lounge," Lynn joked.

"You two work that out." I looked to Deacon, "You need to get your license and I'm sure Lynn will help you. So when do you want to start?"

"How about next Monday? That's a week away, so I can have time to play with my daughter and wife."

"Agreed. Now, go get busy filling out paperwork for your license, so you can start. Don't forget to turn in your resignation with Weber. I'll expect you in bright and early Monday morning."

Lynn looked at Deacon, "Don't worry, Jim never gets here bright and early."

"Thanks, Lynn," I said, then looking to my friends, "What do you say we close up the office and all go to Angelo's for food, my treat. To celebrate our new member."

I called Penny to tell her the news and that she should meet us at Angelo's.

Lacey gathered up Willy, I called to Fred in the back and we all went in the company van to Angelo's. I was feeling excited as I drove over. It was good to have a family.

THE END

~~*~~

Jim Richards Family of Readers

Thanks to the following people who are now part of the Jim Richards Family of Readers. They have read a book or more and enjoyed them. They all volunteered to be included in the list. If you are a fan of the books, send me your full name and you will be included in future books. Send your name to murdernovels@bobmoats.com to be added here and on the website.

* Achim Feifel * Al Norris * Alex Wheatley * Alexandra Delporte-Wilkinson * Amy Tapia * Andrea Bryan * Anne Shepherd * Arianda Sugar * Arlene Markowski * Ashley Augustus * Audra Hall * Barbara Hughes * Barbara Sammons * Barbara Schuler * Barbara Zirger * Beth Donohue Plenskofski * Betsy Childress * Beth Gibson * Bill Sandy * Bill Tornquist * Billie-jo Collie * Boni J Rychener * Carl Bishopric * Carla Lewis * Carole Henderson * Carolyn Conroy * Carolyn Riddle-Linington * Cassy Bailey * Chad Hudson * Charlotte L Duran * Cheryl L. Everett * Cindy Ackley Nunn * Cindy Valstad * Connie Bancroft * Corinne Kay O'Daniel * Dana Robbins Chuchran * Dana Wichita * Danielle Monique * Darren Heald * Dave Travers * David Wilkinson * DeAnn Jannereth * Deanna Miller * Deb Breuker Balbo * Debbie Carter * Debbie White * Deborah Fartuch * Deborah Gauze * Deborah Sullivan * Dee King * Denise Freeman * Diana Carver * Dixie Beck * Donna Gould * Donna Thompson * Donny Minter * Doris Kight * Eddie Moore

Bob Moats

* Eric Walters * Felicia Annette Bradfield * Francine Menor * Gail Chesney * Georgiann Minster * George Conner * Greg Colucci * Hayley Rankin * Harold Garcia * Heidi Arnold * Irma Ranee Coy * Jacqueline Moss * Jan Kimball * Janice Schneider * Janice Spoor * Jennifer Redmond * Jessica Keown-Belous * Jim Beck * Jo Boguslaw * Jo Turner * Joanne Marie Turner * John Peiffer * John Wisbiski * Joseph Wauro * Joyce Stacy * Joyce Trifiletti * Judy Franklin * Judy Travers * Judy Padgett * Julie Heath * Junnahvee Benson * Karen Dahl * Karen Grams * Karen Higham * Karen Kaiser * Karen Meinburg Richwine * Karen Kirkman Parker * Karin Hawkins * Kathleen Donohue Roesing * Kathleen Riddle-Wolfe * Kathy Hinds Moore * Kathy Jones * Kathy Mitchell * Katie Benzler * Kay Burns * Kelly Garcia * Ken Boggs * Keota Rodriguez * Kiera Mccarthy * Kim Estes * Kitty Stolle * Kristie Sciler * Kirsty Stanton * LaLonnie Scallen * Larry Morris * Leann Parr * Lenora Scales * Leslie Marie Jackson * Linda Forester * Linda Ingle Cox * Linda Kennerö * Linda Magill * Lisa Bower * Liz Gibson * Lorraine Wiman * Loretta Alexander * Lynda Bowles * Lynette Lawrance * LuAnn Louttit * Manny Rothman * Marcia Gibson DeWitt * Marie Calder * Marlene Bryan * MaryLouise Kramp * Mary Lynn Gross * Megan Atkins * Meghan Hyden * Melody Cannavan * Michael Carruthers * Michael Vannoy * Michelle Burns-Mitchell * Michelle Pilcher * Micki Potter * Mike Moats * Mimi Baur * Myrna Hecht * Nadine Sutton * Natalie Quine * Neena Martin * O'Della Wilson * Pat Pollington * Pat Rohn * Patricia Jarmon * Patricia C Trezza * Patrick Barry * Paul Lawrance * Peggy Davis * Phyllis Bassett * Raylene Matheny * Rebecca Collins Besner * Renee Brumley * Reta Hanna * Reta Moats * Roberta Navarro-Harder * Sally Berneathy * Sally Hubler * Sarah Santos * Satka Nikc * Sharon E.

Wiseguy Murders

Edwards * Sharon Mangini * Sharon McMillon * Sheena Rawl * Sherry Amstutz * Shirley Alvarez * Shirley Davies * Shirley Williams * Stacie Rowe * Stephanie Conner * Steve Cullen * Susan Haughton * Susan Hesse Adams * Susan Salomon * Suzan K Chase * Taisha Cullum * Tamara Moore * Tammy Castleberry * Tammy Lynn Wood * Ted Murphy * Terri Atkins * Terri Creech * Terry Raab * Tonia Rachael Riggs-Williams * Travis Fleury-Lopez * Twyla Gawlas * Val Brooks * Walt Munsel * Yvonne Isakson *

Thank you to all these wonderful people.

Thank you for purchasing this book. I hope you enjoy it as much as I enjoyed writing it for my faithful readers. Please feel free to email me to tell me what you thought about my stories. I love hearing from the readers. I can be reached at murdernovels@bobmoats.com thanks again!

*